FIRE'S MATE

CHARYBDIS STATION: BOOK 2

C. W. GRAY

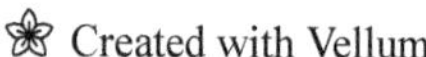 Created with Vellum

CHAPTER 1

ANCHOR'S REST SYSTEM, CHARYBDIS STATION

Fire and his guinea pig, Jellybean, were curled up in the middle of the large, comfortable bed with their friends. It had been a long morning, and Fire needed to recharge, so they had made a cozy nest of pillows, and sleep was fast approaching.

Marmalade, a large orange tabby cat, watched him with sleepy green eyes. She was an expert napper and had taught Fire the importance of finding just the right spot for prime napping potential.

Closer, she thought and sent him an image of them cuddled together. Fire wiggled over and Marmalade nestled against his shoulder so he could settle his head on her. Jellybean moved to lean against the cat's side, and she wrapped a paw around him.

Fire's other friend, Gretty, was already asleep. The little hybrid toddler was fast becoming an expert napper too. She curled against his stomach, and the bushy tail poking out of her diaper tickled his arm.

Fire stared at the tunnel tubes lining the wall of the bedroom. Small balls of fur bustled through the tubing, traveling quickly between rooms in the house. Years ago, the Druffle had been one small nest belonging to Fire's friend Leti. After five years of expansions, there were Druffle nests in every house in the neighborhood and several others on Charybdis Station.

Fire and Marmalade enjoyed watching them. He thought they were adorable, but Marmalade just thought they looked tasty.

Expand the nest. Expand the nest.

Fire chuckled softly. "Silly Druffle want to take over the station, Marmalade."

She patted his nose with her paw. *Sleep. Rest. No worry.*

"Good idea," he whispered and closed his eyes.

The door to the bedroom opened and made him open his eyes again. Lucas looked around, face frantic. When the Betonize-Cardinal hybrid noticed them on the bed, he instantly relaxed.

"Damn it, Fire. What did I tell you about taking Gretty from her room without telling me?" Lucas asked, glaring at him. His silky black feline ears were flat against his head.

Fire hugged Gretty closer. "I left a note."

Lucas held up a piece of red candy. "You left a cinnamon ball."

"Hmm, give me." Fire held his hand out, instantly wanting the hot candy.

Lucas rolled his eyes and sat on the side of the bed before handing the candy to Fire.

"Why are you in my bed?" Lucas asked, smoothing a hand over Gretty's dark, messy hair.

"It was Marmalade's idea. She said Gretty needed to nap with us too, and this is the most comfortable bed," Fire said, pouting around the candy in his mouth.

Truth, Marmalade thought, yawning wide and settling in to sleep.

"You can't blame Marmalade all the time," Lucas said, giving him a look.

"It's the truth," Fire muttered, feeling the grumpiness he'd been hoping to nap away return. "Go away. I need this nap."

Lucas patted his shoulder. "What's wrong?"

"I don't want to talk about it," Fire said and pushed his face into Marmalade's fur. A second later, he looked back at Lucas. "Okay, so this morning, I saw Silas and Rune kissing at the tram before they left for work."

Lucas gave him a gentle smile. "They kiss all the time. They're mates."

"I want a mate." Fire narrowed his eyes. "Almost everyone has a mate but me. Even Estella and Mo are mates, and they don't even know it yet! It's not fair."

Lucas covered his ears. "I didn't hear that. I don't need to know they're mates, or I'll have to tell Morgan and he'll kill Mo. Estella's his little girl, no matter how old she gets."

Fire poked his ear. "You're not listening. *I* want my mate. I want someone to love and take care of. I want to make them smile and laugh and hold them when they cry. I want babies too, lots and lots of babies, or maybe we can adopt a kitten and raise it. I like kittens."

"You'll find your mate someday." Lucas gave him a thoughtful look. "You're young, at least in body. You have years left to find a mate and settle down. What about trying your hand at dating while you wait?"

"I did already." Fire made a disgusted sound. "It was horrible, Lucas. I tried, I swear I did."

Lucas's eyes widened, and his tail twitched with agitation. "You tried dating someone? Did you tell Sebastian? Why didn't I know about this? Damn it, I don't like it."

Fire shook his head. "Sebastian didn't want me to go, but I went anyway and didn't tell him about it until I got back. Sebby never lets me have any fun."

"What did you do, Fire?" Lucas asked, expression as growly as his voice.

Fire sighed and scratched the top of Gretty's head. The toddler smiled in her sleep, then snuffled and burrowed closer to him. "I went to a club with Liam."

Lucas's lips flattened into a thin line. "Liam Doney."

Fire nodded. "He used to date Shae, and Shae told me that Liam would be a good practice date." He gave Lucas a solemn look. "He was wrong, Lucas. It was horrible."

"What did the bastard do?" Lucas growled and moved to pace around the room. "I'll get Sebastian, and we'll hunt the fucker down."

"There was no food," Fire said, fighting back unhappy tears at the memory. "The stupid, horrible club had no food, just drinks. What was I supposed to do, Lucas? All Liam wanted to do was drink and dance, but I was hungry. Then, he said something unforgiveable." Fire buried his face back against Marmalade's side. "He said I shouldn't have brought Jellybean with me on a date."

Lucas was quiet for a moment, and Fire peeked up at him. His friend looked like he was holding back laughter.

"That's why it was a horrible date?" Lucas asked, shoulders shaking.

"Yes," Fire hissed. "Why was there no food? It's not right. I was so hungry and had to wait until I got home to eat. Plus, who wouldn't bring Jellybean with them anywhere if they could? He's the best guinea pig alive. Liam Doney is the worse date ever."

Lucas sighed and sat back down on the bed. "One day,

Fire, you're going to make someone a very good mate. Just stay away from Liam Doney, okay?"

Fire sighed and leaned into Lucas's shoulder. "I really need a nap."

~

AN HOUR LATER, FIRE WAS NO CLOSER TO FINDING HIS USUAL peace and contentment. He hated feeling so out of sorts, but sometimes his feelings simmered for a long, long time before he could make sense of them.

There were days he missed being a simple flame on his home world of Genarg. His earliest memories were of burning a path across the planet while Genarg whispered to him. It had been a peaceful and innocent time. *There wasn't a Sebby though,* he thought, frowning. *There wouldn't be a mate there either.*

Fire had wanted a mate ever since he met the absolute best person in all the galaxy – Sebastian. His Sebby was mated to Alois, and they were so happy. Fire wanted that happiness.

He passed the community park and saw Gravy and Perriwinkle cuddled together under a rose bush. Normally, the two dogs went to work with their people, Hack and Alois. Gravy had told him they were taking a romantic day off soon, and today must be that day.

The two dogs licked each other's faces and mumbled sweet nothings to each other. Usually, Fire loved seeing the two happy, but at the moment their joy just made him sad.

Jellybean rolled beside him in his ball as they continued down the street. *Mate come one day.*

"You're right, Jellybean." Fire scowled. "I just gotta be patient, and that isn't any fun."

Fire passed his friend Leti's house and waved at the large Fire Veil dragon basking on the front lawn. Princess Buttercup usually stayed at Leti's side, but someone had to raise the baby dragons that now lived in the neighborhood.

At least Chutney helps, Fire thought and made sure to wave at the big tomcat in the tree too. Chutney's attention was focused on the two baby dragons, Honey and Stardust, romping around the yard.

Chutney nodded to him before hissing at the babies when Honey pushed Stardust a little too hard.

"You're a good daddy, Chutney." Fire laughed when the cat sent him the image of the two babies behaving perfectly. "Good luck with that."

Princess growled and nudged Aagy, making the juvenile dragon hiss.

Aagy gave Fire a pathetic look and ran to him. *Want to play.*

Fire's hands went to his hips. "No playing until your lessons are over. Princess is teaching you to shift sizes. Don't you want to be able to go with Pepper to school when she starts? You can't do that if you're always big."

Aagy moaned and flopped on his side. *It's hard.*

"Sebastian always says that anything worth doing is gonna be hard," Fire said, shaking his finger. "Princess had to learn all this on his own, but you're lucky and have him to help. You better get to work."

Fire noticed someone watching them from the house. Pepper gave Aagy a longing look, sticky hands pressed to the window. *Must be her lunch time*, Fire thought, stomach growling. *I need lunch too.*

Love sister. Aagy slowly got to his feet and went back to Princess, head hanging low. *For sister.*

Princess hissed and smoke curled from his nostrils. *Annoying juvenile.*

"He's trying, Princess," Fire said, hugging the big dragon. "Give him a chance?"

Rather eat him, but Mother likes stupid little one. Princess sighed and nudged Aagy again. *He learn.*

Fire chuckled and looked back at Leti's house. Now, Leti stood with Pepper and watched the dragons. The man had his son Milo on his hip and wore the same look of longing as Pepper. They wanted their dragons to come play with them.

"Princess, maybe you can have a break?" Fire nodded toward the window.

Princess looked up, eyes softening when he saw Leti. *Mother needs me.*

Sister, Aagy said, balancing on his hind legs to watch Pepper. *Playtime?*

Princess grumbled but went to gather the babies before going into the house.

Fire's stomach rumbled so he hurried to his own home next door. "Jellybean, we need lunch."

Sebastian and his apprentice, Kelly, were in the living room studying. Sebastian was a shaman and was training Kelly to be one too. Fire had overheard them talking about learning more defensive skills to better protect the neighborhood.

To the average observer, they looked like they were sitting across from one another, staring at the air above them. Fire let his mind fall into the spirit world, so he could see what they were doing.

Instantly, the world brightened around him and filled with threads connecting everything around him. He admired the strong gold and red thread binding him to Sebastian. He remembered having a similar thread connect him to his queen, but that was a very long time ago, and he didn't like thinking about her. That thread had never been as strong as the one connecting him to Sebastian.

The two shamans were listening to one of Sebastian's spirit guides, Tell, while he explained something about drowning someone in soil. *Boring*, Fire thought, wrinkling his nose and leaving the spirit world, so he wouldn't have to hear Tell drone on and on.

While Fire could see the spirit world, since he was an Element, he couldn't manipulate any of the threads he saw or even do more than talk to a spirit if it happened to show up around him.

A sweet trilling drew his attention, and Fire turned around. Sebastian's bird, Mustachio, watched them from one of his many perches. The large Radollia shimmered in the light.

"Hi, Mustachio," Fire whispered. "I need lunch."

The bird glared at him and used a wing to cover his own plate of fresh vegetables and strips of meat.

"I wasn't gonna take your food," Fire said, rolling his eyes. "I only did that once, and Sebastian got mad."

Fire went and made himself a couple of sandwiches and grabbed a carrot before returning to watch Kelly and Sebastian. He helped Jellybean out of his ball and handed him the carrot before focusing on his own lunch.

Jellybean flopped back against his favorite pillow and nibbled his carrot.

Fire grabbed a pillow and lay down beside him. He ate quickly and sighed when his stomach continued to grumble. *Need more food.*

He made sure Sebastian wasn't looking, then stuck his tongue out at Kelly.

She looked away from Tell and snickered when she saw him.

He made a face and wiggled side to side. *Stupid Kelly.*

She winked and blew a raspberry at him.

"Behave, you two," Sebastian said, turning around to give Fire *the look.*

Fire's shoulders slumped. Kelly really wasn't that bad, but she took a lot of Sebastian's time, and Fire didn't like it. "Sorry."

Sebastian held his arms open, and Fire went in for a hug. Sebastian's aura of calm and love instantly made him feel better.

"How was your nap?" Sebastian asked, rubbing Fire's back.

"Lucas interrupted us and made me talk," Fire grumbled. "I want my mate, Sebby, and maybe a kitten. A kitten would be nice, wouldn't it?"

"Maybe after you mate," Sebastian said, amused. "You have Jellybean."

"I love Jellybean." Fire watched his guinea pig friend roll around on his pillow. "A kitten would love Jellybean too."

Kelly laughed. "Come on, Sebastian. How can you resist that face?"

Sebastian snorted. "Don't you start. We have too much going on for Fire to get a kitten." He held Fire back a little. "We're going somewhere that I think you'll really like."

Fire patted his stomach. "Juniper's Diner? I'm hungry."

"Of course you are," Kelly said, rolling her eyes.

Sebastian bit back his smile. "We'll go there too since it's time for a break. The place I'm talking about is far away. It's a planet called Burnished Outpost."

Fire tilted his head, thinking over what he knew of their system. "That's where Leti's mate is from."

"It's a desert planet," Sebastian said, straightening Fire's mussed hair. "Hack is going there to meet his younger half-siblings. We're all going to go with him, and you'll have a few weeks to play in the heat."

Fire smiled widely, something settling deep within him. "I can't wait."

CHAPTER 2

ANCHOR'S REST SYSTEM, BURNISHED OUTPOST

Quigley watched the sun slowly rise over the sand dunes around the clan's encampment. The bright, fiery orb turned the sand a soft pink, and he had to fight down the urge to grab one of the Oryx and ride toward the sun. His bones told him a sandstorm was coming, though there was barely any wind.

"What's firing up your shorts?" Gram asked him, moving to stand beside him, her hand a welcome weight on his shoulder.

His grandmother was still a beautiful woman, though her face was lined and her hair gray. She used to stand tall and strong, but age and a hard life weighed on her, and her bones hurt more often than not. To him, that didn't matter. She was still his Gram and would always be the most beautiful woman around, her only equals his sister, Sara, and his daughter, Aster.

"Quig, did you hear me, or do I need to yell louder?" Gram asked, voice rising with each word.

Quigley rolled his eyes. "I'm okay, Gram. I'm just feeling the need for a hunt."

She gave him a considering look. "You've been getting that feeling a lot lately. It reminds me of when I felt the mating call. My feet itched like they were on fire, and I practically ran the whole way to your grandfather's clan to find him."

Quigley snorted. "Unless my mate lives in the sky, I'm not feeling any mating call."

"The rumors say the chieftain in Star's Oasis sends our people there," Gram said, pointing into the sky. "Maybe it wouldn't be so bad to go."

Quigley looked around, making sure no one was around them. "They'd never let us go, Gram. You know that. They don't even like it when we go off on a hunt by ourselves."

She gave him a sad look and patted his stomach. "One day, you may not have a choice, Quig. I'll get the kids ready for the hunt."

"Thanks." He turned away from the rising sun and walked toward the clan elder's tent.

Horus lived in the largest tent at the center of the encampment. The man had only been clan elder a few years now, but he had already made changes. *Changes for the worse*, Quigley thought to himself.

The smell of cooked meat filled the air, but the cooking fires were already being doused. The desert heat made cooking on a fire during the day unpleasant to say the least. They cooked breakfast before sunrise and dinner after the sun set.

Horus sat outside his tent, eating his breakfast. "Quigley."

Quigley nodded. He had discovered that with Horus, asking for permission was far worse than simply demanding his agreement. The elder admired strength. "Just letting you know, I'm going on a hunt. I'll be back in a few weeks."

"Are you finally taking those useless bags of stones to the deep desert?" Horus asked, smirking.

He had wanted Quigley to abandon Gram and the rest of his family for years. The man stopped just short of ordering Quigley to do it, but the order was coming soon. Quigley knew it.

"They're still useful." Quigley's voice was gruff, and he hated equating his family to tools to be used, but that was all Horus understood.

"You're the best hunter in the clan," Horus said, giving him a hard look. "You should have settled down with a nice woman and had your own strong children by now. Instead you burden yourself with an old woman and two useless children."

"We take care of ourselves and contribute to the clan," Quigley said, his teeth clenched tightly.

The tent flap opened and Sara stepped out. Quigley's sister was a beautiful woman, tall and strong, her long, dark hair in braids. Just like Quigley, her birth markings were prominent, curving in dark lines along her cheekbones and bare shoulders. Their family had always had a strong link to their inner fire.

She carried her newborn son, Cyrus, in her arms. "Hey, Quig. If you're going on a hunt, will you ask Aster to try to find some Gaora cactus fruit for me?"

Quigley smiled. His sister always tried to remind Horus of how useful Quigley's *bags of stones* really were. Aster may be blind, but she had an uncanny way of tracking. "Sure. We're heading out this morning."

Sara bowed her head to Horus. "Elder, may I walk my brother to his tent?"

Horus waved a hand at her. "Fine. Just be back in an hour. You have a husband to see to."

Quigley and Sara walked in silence at first. He always had to rein in his temper when Horus or Dustin ordered her about. He hated that Sara had agreed to marry the elder's son, but it had been her choice.

"Do you remember when we used to lie in the sands at night and look at the stars?" Sara asked, finally breaking the silence. "Grandfather used to tell us all about the constellations. He taught us how to follow them, but he also taught us their stories."

Quigley smiled and nudged Sara with his shoulder. "Gram and I have been teaching Aster and David."

"I want that for Cyrus," Sara whispered. "I want him to grow up like we did."

Quigley arched a brow. "You married Dustin."

She looked away. "You know why I did."

"I didn't ask you to do that, Sara." Quigley took a deep breath, trying to let go of his anger. "I didn't ask you to try to protect me. No one knows about *you know what,* and they never will."

She looked around, eyes panicked. "Be quiet. You never know who's listening. Quigley, you're my brother, and I will always do what I can to protect you. I thought marrying Dustin would give our family some protection from the elder's vile laws, but I was wrong. He won't stand up for his family, little less his in-laws."

"What happened?" Quigley asked, voice low.

Sara licked her lips and gave him a worried look. "He's going to find out about Cyrus. He offered to change his diaper yesterday, and I know it was only to look at his stomach."

Quigley paled. "You think Dustin will leave him to the gods in the deep desert?"

"I think he'll kill him on the spot," Sara said, voice

hoarse.

"We need to leave. Now." Quigley frowned. He always packed up his household when they went on a hunt. He couldn't trust the clan to watch out for them if he wasn't there. That wouldn't call attention to them.

"You go first," Sara whispered. "Wait for me at Aster's spot. I'll sneak out tonight after Dustin goes to sleep. I'll bring Cyrus, and we'll meet you there."

Quigley looked up at the clear sky again. "A sandstorm is coming. You need to leave earlier."

Sara nodded, not even questioning him. She knew his bones didn't lie. "I'll do what I can."

"I'll pack food and water for you. Don't bring more than your Oryx can carry."

They stopped in front of the spot his tent normally stood. Gram and the kids already had it packed up and their Oryx ready to go.

"Hi, Aunt Sara." Aster smiled toward them. She already sat atop her own mount and wore her hunting clothes. Her black hair was pulled back in a long braid, and her hand rested on her hunting knife.

Sara gave her a fond look. "Good morning, dearest."

His adopted daughter had been born blind. When her birth parents decided to leave her in the deep desert, Quigley had stepped forward and taken her in. That was ten years ago, and Aster had proven she was more than capable of surviving with the love of a family.

"Are you coming with, Aunt Sara?" David asked. Quigley's son was just climbing on his own Oryx. He was another child that was to be left to the gods. He had been born without any of the birth markings that were common amongst the Burnished. He would never be able to access his inner fire without them, so he was deemed too weak for survival.

Quigley smiled at his son. That had been seven years ago, and David was doing just fine. Like Aster, he was a valuable member of Quigley's family simply by existing. The fact that he was good with a throwing knife and took care of the Oryx was just a bonus.

Sara patted his leg and looked around nervously. "Maybe next time. Go pick out one of the goats to take with you, sweet boy. You'll need the milk. Tell the herd master that I gave you permission."

David gave her a curious look, then slid down. "Okay. I'll take good care of her for you."

"I know you will," Sara said, kissing the top of his head.

David ran toward the herds, and Gram gave them both a look before taking Cyrus from Sara and cuddling him. "Why the serious face, Sara girl? Wish you were going with us?"

"More than anything," Sara said, eyes closing.

"We're leaving for good," Quigley said, voice low. "Cyrus's safety is at risk."

Gram's eyes widened in understanding. "Alright then. We'll go to Star's Oasis. The Burnished Chieftain doesn't have the same prejudices as our clan elder."

"That's the only safe place," he said.

"I need to get back before Dustin gets angry," Sara said and bit her lip. "Maybe, when we're at Star's Oasis, you can finally meet someone and settle down. I want to see you happy, Quig. I want to see you try to flirt and deal with all the awkwardness of courting."

"Why would you want to see that?" Quigley laughed and pulled Sara into a hug. "Be careful, little sister. I'll see you soon."

AFTER A DAY OF SUCCESSFUL HUNTING, QUIGLEY LED HIS family to the small, hidden cave that Aster had discovered a few years ago. His daughter had a way of finding the desert's secrets that Quigley didn't fully understand.

As the sun set, Aster worked on starting a fire, while Gram and Quigley unloaded the Oryx. They had a couple of bags of Gaora cactus fruit and two jackrabbits, which would make for a good dinner and breakfast.

"Come on, Gracie," David said, tugging the lead for the small goat Sara had sent with them. "Let's get you in the shade."

The black and brown goat followed along placidly, adoring eyes focused on Quigley's son.

Quigley grinned. "I think the goat's part of the family now."

"That boy of yours has a soft heart." Gram patted the side of her Oryx, Nadine. "Just like us."

Quigley took a moment to scratch his own Oryx's long ears. Cactus had been with him a long time. "I wouldn't have it any other way."

Gram's long robe blew hard against her legs, and she gave Quigley a concerned look. "That storm's definitely coming."

He looked out over the desert, noting the sand bouncing on the ground. "Sara should be on her way. She said she'd leave as early as possible."

"I'm worried about her." Gram set a bag down near the fire, then went back for another. "If Horus and Dustin find out the baby has a birthing line, they'll kill him. It took a lot to hide your birthing line from your father, that's for sure. If they're already suspicious, they'll be watching."

Aster tilted her head. "Cyrus is like you, Dad?"

"Unfortunately." Quigley set the last bag down and pulled the Oryx into the mouth of the cave.

"I like the dots you have on your tummy," David said, hugging Quigley around the waist. "The gods made you special so you could have babies. There's nothing wrong with that."

Quigley picked his son up and hugged him tight. "I like that idea, son. Thank you."

Aster's giggles echoed across the cavern. "The gods didn't make him that way, David, offworlder blood did. Remember? Gram told us that once Burnished Outpost had all kinds of species living here, and they mated with the Burnished. Dad can have babies because of his ancestry."

David rolled his eyes. "Whatever. He's still special and so is Cyrus."

Gram chuckled and patted his shoulder. "Why don't you take watch, Quig? We'll ready the camp and make dinner."

Quigley squeezed David one more time, then set him on his feet. "Good idea. It shouldn't be more than a few hours before Sara gets here. She'll be riding the storm in."

He went to the mouth of the cave and climbed up and over the rocks around it. Sara would be coming in from the east, using the stars to guide her.

He looked up at the night sky. Two moons shone bright against the deep black. The small, golden moon was called Helara, the blessed sanctuary where all the abandoned supposedly went. The larger moon, Braxia, glowed an eerie, dark purple. Gram had told him that once it held all the Burnished gods, but now lay abandoned.

Quigley didn't know what he believed. He knew what he saw – a sky full of stars and two glowing moons. He knew the planets too – Grellweir, Cardinal Hold, Siren's Lament, Fallow, and Haven.

Gram had told them stories of how the Burnished once traveled among the stars and planets. He wasn't sure he believed that any more than he believed in the glorious paradise of Helara.

A few hours later, the wind had picked up and the sand danced on the ground in the light of the moons. Quigley knew they had less than an hour before the storm hit.

Gram held her hand over her eyes as she came to stand by him. "We've pulled the Oryx into the cave and barricaded as well as we can."

"I'm going to ride out a bit, but I'll be back before the storm hits." He headed back to the cave. "She should be here already."

"I'll keep the children safe," Gram said, helping him get Cactus ready to ride.

Quigley hopped onto his Oryx and rode fast toward the east, eyes searching for shadows against the pale sand.

It took him a half hour to find them. One lone Oryx rode fast toward him with at least thirty others chasing behind.

"No." Quigley urged Cactus toward Sara.

As soon as he reached her, he turned and ran beside her. "What happened?" he asked, the wind grabbing his words. Somehow, they still made it to her.

"I killed Horus," she yelled. "I heard them saying they would kill Cyrus, so I poisoned dinner. Dustin didn't die, but Horus did. They won't stop coming for me, Quig."

"We'll lose them in the storm," he yelled back.

"No." The faint moonlight glinted in Sara's eyes. "There are too many, and my Oryx is exhausted."

She rode closer and tossed him the bag she had strapped to her back.

Quigley yelped, fumbling to catch it. He could feel little Cyrus inside. "Damn it, Sara, I almost dropped him."

"You always caught me when I fell." Sara's eyes watered. "I'll hold them off while you get to Aster's spot. Take care of him, Quig. Tell him the stories of the stars and love him as your own."

"Not happening," Quigley yelled back, strapping Cyrus's bag around his front. Panic filled him at Sara's stubborn expression. He knew that look. "I'm not leaving you."

"I'm not the one who can get us to Star's Oasis." She loosened the cinch of her saddle. "I *can* keep them away from our family."

"Sara, don't –"

She tossed him the reins of her Oryx, then swung off his back, rolling into the sand.

He looked back and saw her fire igniting in the murky, dusty night air. The birthmarks lining her body went from black to a fiery red. The shadows following them lit up as the other Burnished called to their own flames. Compared to Sara, they were a weak imitation.

Sara screamed, and her fire grew bright as she sent flames dancing toward the mob.

Cyrus whimpered in his carrier, and Quigley closed his eyes. He wanted to stay. He wanted to fight beside his sister.

Cyrus whimpered again. Quigley opened his eyes and focused on the stars above to lead him back to his family. His body shook as he tried to hold back his sobs. *Sara.*

The sandstorm grew stronger, and soon he couldn't see any flames behind him and very few stars in the sky. He almost passed the cave, but David called out to him.

"Dad, we're here," he said, waving his arms.

Quigley pulled the Oryx to a stop, and David was there in an instant to take their reins and pull them into the cave.

He slid from Cactus's back, bracing a hand on Cyrus's back through the bag.

Gram stared at Sara's Oryx for a moment, eyes watering. "She's not coming, is she?"

Quigley wiped at the tears making trails through the dust on his face. "She held them back so we could get away."

Cyrus whimpered again, working his way up to a wail.

"I'll get him some milk," David said, voice breaking as tears filled his eyes.

Aster covered her mouth, holding back a moan. She moved to Quigley's side, and he wrapped his arm around her. Gram pulled David with her, and a moment later, they clung together as they cried.

THE NEXT MORNING, QUIGLEY RODE BACK TO THE battlefield. Riderless Oryx milled around and seared bodies were half buried in the sand. He knew the survivors hadn't lingered here during the storm. If they had, there would have been a lot more dead.

He found her after a moment. Her body was burned badly, her eyes open and unseeing.

Quigley fell to his knees beside her, fighting back fresh tears. Her body was stiff as he pulled her close for one last hug. "I swear I'll protect him, Sara. I swear on the stars and Helara that he'll always be safe."

He forced himself to lay her down and step back. He watched a wisp of her hair blow in the wind and held his hands over her body, calling his hottest flames to his hands. His birthmarks glowed almost white as the flames covered Sara's body.

A few moments later, her ashes mixed with the desert sand.

Quigley closed his eyes and pictured her laughing face. He would remember her that way. He would remember her as his strong, beautifully brave sister.

CHAPTER 3

ANCHOR'S REST SYSTEM, BURNISHED OUTPOST

Fire pressed his face to the window and watched as the white sandstone spaceport grew closer. Star's Oasis was in the middle of a desert, and Fire couldn't wait to feel the hot sand between his toes.

Jellybean squeaked from where he rode on Fire's shoulder. *You like?*

"I love it, Jellybean," he said, breath moistening the window. "I can feel the heat from here."

"You're going to run as soon as we land, aren't you?" Sebastian asked, amused.

Fire nodded and bumped his head on the window. "Will you watch Jellybean?"

Sebastian picked up the guinea pig and tucked him against his chest. "I'll take care of him. Make sure you're back by sundown or I'll worry."

"I will." Fire looked over his shoulder. Hack, Leti, and all their kids gathered behind them. "Hack needs us."

Coming back to Burnished Outpost after years of being gone was hard for Leti's mate. The man hadn't had a good life while he was there and had even been abandoned by his mother. Fire knew the only reason Hack had come back at all was to meet his three youngest half-brothers.

I'll never abandon my babies, he thought and reached over to pet Jellybean. "I love you, Jellybean."

Love you. Jellybean squeaked and wiggled in Sebastian's arms. *Want to run with you.*

"We'll go for a run together tomorrow, Jellybean. This run is gonna be fast, and I don't want you to get hurt. Sebby will let you roll with him though." Fire hurried and got Jellybean's ball ready.

Sebastian sighed and put the wiggling guinea pig into the ball. "Now I have three kids to watch over while we're here."

Alois, Sebastian's mate, grunted from beside him. He had their youngest, Mordy, strapped to his chest, and Nina, their eldest, held his hand. "Hello, love. I'm right here."

Sebastian gave him an exaggerated look of surprise. "Oh yeah. I actually have four kids."

Alois scowled but pulled Sebastian into his side. "Nina and I won't get up to too much trouble."

"Only because Mordecai is there to keep you in line," Sebastian said, smiling softly.

Mordy grunted, sounding a lot like his papa. He swung his legs and grinned at them.

Fire pushed back the nasty ball of envy that upset his stomach. *I'll find my own mate one day.*

The Blue Solace landed in the spaceport and everyone started grabbing their bags. They would be staying for a week, so Fire had made sure to pack extra snacks.

He hurried and grabbed Hack's bag before the man could, then gave the big Burnished a hug. "It's gonna be okay, Hack. Siblings aren't so bad." Fire paused. "Well, I don't really have a sibling, so maybe they are bad. Death is kinda like my brother and friend both, and he's okay. He's my brother friend and Jellybean is my best friend." Fire giggled hard enough to almost drop Hack's bag.

Hack groaned and hugged Fire tightly until his giggles stopped. "Thanks, Fire."

Fire started to reply, but the cargo ramp lowered and he felt a gust of heat. "Gotta go!"

He ran past Kelly and dropped his own bag, along with Hack's, at her feet.

She gave him an amused glare. "Yeah, I'll just take care of these."

"Good," he yelled over his shoulder and ran down the ramp.

Fire pulled his clothes and shoes off as he ran past the gathered Burnished officials, ignoring their startled shouts.

As soon as he was naked, he shifted into his elemental form, human body twisting and burning away into flames. After that, he was lost to the heated desert sands.

It reminded him of the deserts of Genarg. He remembered the planet calling to him and deepening his awareness long before he was given a body.

All of that was eons ago, and he'd taken many forms since then, but his elemental form always brought back that feeling of wild freedom. While this planet didn't speak to him like Genarg, it was still a comforting presence in the back of his mind.

As he moved farther away from Star's Oasis, the bare shrubs and cacti grew scarce, and the animals were harder to spot.

A skinny jackrabbit hopped behind a bush. It looked like a much smaller version of Fire's friend Abbot. Mo had found Abbot as a baby right here on Burnished Outpost.

Hours passed as he raced across the beautiful desert, and he lost track of his direction. He spotted the occasional traveler but kept far away from them. Sebastian had told him that the Burnished outside of Star's Oasis may not be friendly.

A spark of light reflecting off metal caught his attention, and he darted toward it, curious.

A small group of travelers rode large, long-eared mounts down a sand dune. Two of the riders were children, and the youngest even had a goat tied to the back of his mount. The boy and girl looked frightened, and he didn't like it.

The third rider was an older woman, face lined with worry and pain. She pulled the reins of several more of the mounts behind her, but he could tell her hands were hurting.

Fire's attention focused on the last rider, and he froze in the air. The man was one of the Burnished with long, narrow, pointed ears and dark skin. His birthmarks were different than Hack's though. Leti's mate's marks were jagged and sharply angled. This man's markings were curved and elegant, somehow appearing softer.

He looked to be in his late thirties or early forties, and the man's face was a rough contrast to his delicate markings. His black hair was cut close to his head, and a long scar cut across one of his eyebrows.

Mate. The word echoed through every particle of Fire's being, and the planet beneath him grew warmer as the knowledge seeped into his soul. It approved.

It took a moment for Fire to notice the bundled infant strapped to his mate's chest. Curious, Fire flew closer, circling them from high above.

His mate's group reached the bottom of the dune, and the woman called out, "Quig, they've seen us!"

"Fuck," the man said, teeth grinding together. "Aster, take Cyrus. Gram keep heading north. We're still a week out from Star's Oasis, but you can get them there."

"Dad, no," the girl gasped as she fumbled to hold bundled infant. Fire only then noticed her eyes were darker and unfocused. "Don't leave us."

His mate – Quig, the woman had called him – handed the baby to the girl. "I'm sorry, sunrise, but I have to stop them." He looked at the boy. "David."

The boy ducked his face, tears falling hard. "We love you, Dad. We'll take care of Cyrus. I swear."

Quig looked at the three kids, dark eyes so sad that Fire wanted to hug him and never let go. "I love you too. All of you."

He turned his mount around and made the hard trek back up the sand dune.

Fire followed him and finally noticed the large group of riders growing closer.

Quig leaned forward and patted his mount's neck before sliding off the creature. "Get back to them, Cactus. Watch over my kids, okay?"

The mount bleated softly, sounding a lot like Leti's goat, Trixie. Cactus didn't move from Quig's side, no matter how loudly the man yelled at him.

"I don't want you to die, Cactus. Please go." His mate was near tears, and Fire couldn't take it.

Fire landed between his mate and the approaching riders. He shifted to his human form, uncaring that he was naked. He frowned, feeling the malice coming from the riders. *What would Fluffle do?* he thought, quickly counting the riders. *Fluffle would go for the throat.*

"You can't have my mate!" Fire held his hands out. Flames danced around him and spread to the sides, making a long, flaming barrier. He let the heat grow, burning with a white light.

The riders came to a stop at his flame barrier and watched it spread out, east and west.

One of the men dismounted and watched him through the flames. "Who are you to stand between me and my enemy?"

Fire glared at him. "I've seen your type all across the galaxy. You're a big, stupid bully, and I won't let you hurt them. They're mine now, all of them, and you won't touch them."

He called the flames higher, and they shot into the sky.

The man stepped back as the heat grew.

Fire made sure the man was watching him before speaking again. "You better go away."

The man looked past Fire. "This isn't over, Quigley. The child dies along with you and all of your broken family."

Fire growled and focused his power. A large, fiery creature grew from the flames. He formed it to resemble the toughest being he knew: Fluffle. A large, fluffy housecat made of flames surveyed the riders below her, then roared, spewing flames above them.

The riders shouted, fear clear on their faces, as their mounts startled and bucked.

The man across the barrier hurried back to his mount. "Retreat! Quickly!"

Fire smiled as he sent the mock Fluffle after them, ordering his creation to nip at their heels until they were far away.

The barrier of flames remained, and Fire blew it a kiss, ordering the flames to stay there. It would make it hard for the riders to catch up to his new friends.

"What are you?" Quigley asked, awe filling his voice.

Fire turned around and hurried to his mate's side. He ducked under the man's arm and hugged him. "Wow, you're taller from the ground. You're even taller than Hack and he's big. Are you Quigley? I'm Fire and I'm your mate."

"Family call me Quig." Quigley licked his lips, eyes wide. "Mate. You're really my mate."

Fire nuzzled the bare skin at the base of Quigley's throat. "You smell really good." He licked him. "Hmm, you taste good too."

Quigley swallowed hard and stepped up, holding Fire away from him. "You're naked."

"Yep." Fire looked down, feeling his dick stir. "Hey, look! That didn't happen when I went out with Liam Doney."

Quigley's eyes narrowed, his face growing fierce. "Who's Liam Doney?"

Fire pointed at his dick. "Focus, Quig. I've never gotten to have sex in any of my cycles, and it's supposed to be really good."

Quigley's lips twitched up. He went to his mount and dug through one of the packs before pulling out a pair of loose, white pants and a long, tan, sleeveless tunic.

He tossed them to Fire. "We need to catch up to my family."

Fire's lip trembled, and he looked down at his erection. "Really?"

Quigley's laughter rumbled around Fire, making him shiver. "Come meet my family."

Fire squealed and hurried into his clothes. "I saw them. You have a Gram and three children. I was just telling Sebby that I wanted babies, and now I'll have three. I didn't even think about having a Gram. Is she nice? What do you do with a Gram exactly? Hack and Leti have a Grandpa Moses, and he spends a lot of time with the kids while they're working. Is that what Gram will do?"

Quigley caught Fire as he started to topple, legs caught in his pants. "One thing at a time, mate. Clothes first."

Fire nodded and grinned. "Clothes, then family, then sex."

Quigley gave him a half smile and helped him pull up his pants. "Sex is important, huh?"

Fire shrugged. "I think so. I was never interested in it until recently."

Quigley brushed a thumb across Fire's cheekbone. "Gram told me that finding your lifemate is like finding an oasis when you've been out of water for two days. She says the world suddenly comes alive."

Fire gasped and pushed his face into Quigley's hand. "Is that what's happening? All I can feel is happy. I've wanted a person of my own for a long time, and now you're here. I'm going to take such good care of you. I promise."

Quigley swallowed hard. "I think Gram was right. Come on. I'll help you get on Cactus."

Fire hugged Quigley one more time, then ran over to the funny looking mount. "I've never seen an animal like you. Hi, Cactus. I'm Fire and I'm your person's mate. We're going to be friends, okay? I'll introduce you to Jellybean, Fluffle, Princess Buttercup, and all the other pets. You'll like them."

He felt the animal's mind brush against his, but until they got to know one another, Fire knew he wouldn't be able to talk to him.

Fire hugged the mount. "Don't worry. We'll spend lots of time together."

Quigley cleared his throat, his dark eyes full of amusement. "Are you done hugging my Oryx?"

"Not yet," Fire said and patted Cactus's nose. "Making friends takes time, Quig. Don't worry though. I'll show you how it's done."

CHAPTER 4

Quigley pushed Cactus hard, hurrying to catch up with Gram and the kids. It bothered him to think that they believed him to be dead. *I thought I was dead too*, he thought, still a little unsure that he wasn't imagining the man riding behind him.

Fire's arms were wrapped around him and his chin nestled on Quigley's shoulder. "Jellybean likes running in his ball, but you have to watch how fast you go. He gets upset if you leave him behind. It wasn't so bad when Marshmallow was alive because she ran at his pace, but she's passed on. Now, she's a ghost guinea pig and guards Seshi. He lives down the road, by the way."

Quigley's mate had been talking from the moment they left the fire barrier, and Quigley didn't understand even half of what Fire was saying. *I'll figure it out*, he thought with a smile, enjoying the excitement and joy in his mate's voice.

My mate. His eyes watered as he thought of what Sara would say. It had been a month since she'd died, and there wasn't a day that went by where he didn't think of her. *She would adore my mate.*

Fire was an odd-looking young man, with short, rounded ears, light skin, and yellow hair. He had no markings like the Burnished, but he certainly had a fire. He *was* fire. Even if Quigley hadn't seen what Fire could do, his eyes gave him away. They swirled with golden flames, looking much like the Burnished's eyes did when pulling from their inner fire.

Quigley hadn't known what he was seeing when he first saw his mate in what he called his elemental form. Fire had been a twisting, ever-moving ribbon of flames. When he had shifted and created the barrier, flames had surrounded him, curling against him like a lover, but leaving his soft skin untouched.

Soft, naked skin. Quigley couldn't wait to get his hands on his mate, but he found himself reluctant to move quickly. In the past, his sexual encounters had been hurried embraces hidden in the shadows. His clan elder would never have accepted a man loving another man, and Quigley couldn't risk anyone seeing his birthing line in any case.

With Fire, Quigley wanted to take his time. He wanted to learn everything about his mate.

"Sebastian saved me, so he's like my favorite person in the whole world," Fire said, next to his ear. "He protects me and loves me. His mate, Alois, does too. They'll let us live in their attic forever if we want. I like to play with Nina and Mordy too. You'll like them. Nina is really smart and knows how to get the candy jar open. Mordy snores really loud when he naps, but he likes to snuggle so that's good. Then there's Periwinkle, Mustachio, and Mocha. They're good friends, but they spend a lot of time away. Peri loves Gravy, who lives next door, and Mocha spends a lot of time with Alois. Mustachio, of course, goes everywhere with Sebastian. I told them that I want a cat, but now I have three babies, so I think I can wait on a cat."

Quigley grinned, not understanding why anyone would name a person Gravy. *Offworlders are different, right? Don't think too hard on it.*

It took them a little less than an hour to catch up to Gram and the kids.

When Gram saw him, she pulled the Oryx to a stop and slid off Nadine. "Quig!"

Quigley barely had time to dismount before she was in his arms. "I'm here, Gram. I'm so sorry that had to happen."

"I thought we'd lost you too." She buried her face against his chest.

Aster and David ran to him, and he pulled Gram down so he could brace for their hug.

"You're alive," Aster said, holding Cyrus between them so she could hug him. "How?"

"It doesn't matter how," David said, body shaking with his sobs. "Don't leave us again, Daddy. Okay?"

Quigley held them to him for a long while, his cheek balanced on Gram's head. He watched Fire watching them. *Thank you*, he mouthed the words.

Fire nodded, tears falling, as he grinned widely. Quigley's mate had saved his life, and he would never be able to repay him for that.

"Who's that?" Aster asked, waving toward Fire. "He feels different than us."

Fire's eyes grew round. "You can *feel* me? Am I a good feeling? Like when I eat a whole pie and curl up with Marmalade for a nap?" His eyes heated as he looked Quigley up and down. "Maybe it's like when I'm pressed against Quig and my–"

"Please just answer him, Aster," Quigley interrupted, face heating with embarrassment and a little bit of arousal.

Gram watched him, eyes dancing with humor. "I want to know what he was going to say."

"Me too," David said, twisting around to look at Fire.

"No, you don't," Aster said, wincing. "I think he's Dad's mate, and you know what newly mated people do all the time."

David made a face. "Sex."

Fire came to them, body completely at ease. "Your dad makes my–"

Quigley covered Fire's mouth with his hand. "This is Fire. He's my mate. He saved me from the clan."

"Are you an offworlder?" David asked, eyes focused on Fire's ears. "If your ears are just broken, it's okay. We'll still love you."

Fire licked Quigley's palm, making him jump and move his hand. "Thank you, David, but my ears are okay. My body is human. Mostly."

Gram tilted her head and frowned. "Your body?"

Fire shrugged. "It's kinda a long story, and I want to cuddle with Quig some more. Can I tell you tonight?"

Quigley flushed and pulled Fire into the hug. "That sounds like a plan. The clan won't come for us anytime soon, but Star's Oasis is still a long way away. Let's ride."

David sighed and pulled away to run to his Oryx. "Hurry, everyone. I want to hear the story."

Gram kissed the side of Quigley's head and stood. "I don't care what you are, Fire. You saved my grandson. Welcome to the family."

Fire's eyes glistened. "I have a Gram. Quig, I have a Gram."

Quigley chuckled and brushed Fire's hair back from his face. "You may not want her when you get to know her. Gram is a pain in the ass."

Gram snorted and mounted her Oryx. "Just for that, I'll lead and you pull the other Oryx behind us."

"I'll do it," Fire said, bouncing in place. "I need to get to know them."

He hugged Aster and Cyrus and watched Fire hurry to gather the lose reins of the spare Oryx they travelled with.

"Whatever he is, he's ancient," Aster said quietly. "I can feel the age on him."

She handed him Cyrus. The baby was grumpy from the heat and constant motion of the Oryx, but he settled down when Quigley strapped him to his chest.

"What else do you feel?" he asked, curious.

"He feels like love and wildness," Aster whispered. "He feels like my love for you, Gram, and David. How you felt for Aunt Sara. How Gram felt about Grampa. The love you feel for Cactus and the other Oryx, even if you don't like admitting it. He feels like all of that, Dad, but he also feels like dancing around the fire at night as Gram tells us the stories of the stars. He feels like racing down a dune with David to see who has to clean up from dinner." She smiled softly. "Love and wildness. I've never met anyone like him."

"Me neither," he whispered, watching Fire pet Gracie and talk to David. "I wish I could feel people the way you do."

"You've always told me every person has their gifts." Aster's voice grew rough. "Dad, we can't lose you. Okay? We need you to hold us together. David thought you'd come back. He acted like he didn't, but he had hope. Gram and me thought you were dead. We can't go through that again."

He pressed his forehead to hers. "I can't promise you that I'll never die, sunrise. Everyone dies. I can promise you that as long as I live, I will fight to stay with you."

Aster stroked his cheek, then nodded. "I love you, Dad."

"Love you too." He stroked Cyrus's covered head and

watched Aster go straight to her Oryx and mount. His children were both so special, and it humbled him every day to get to be their father.

Cyrus cooed and looked up at him. The tips of the baby's ears twitched, and he wiggled his tiny fist at Quigley. His faint markings looked just like Sara's, and Quigley suspected they would darken to a deep black like most of his family's did.

"It will be okay, Cy," he whispered. "You are well protected."

Fire skipped back to him. "Can I carry the baby? Is he our son too? What's his name?"

Quigley's mouth opened and closed a few times as he struggled to find the right words. "Cyrus is my nephew, but now I'll raise him as my son. Our son? Are you sure you want that?"

Fire took Cyrus out of his carrier and cuddled him close. "Mates share their family. That's how it works. Gram is mine. Aster is mine. David is mine. Cyrus is mine. All of you are mine. Even Gracie."

"You are… You honor me, Fire." Quigley helped him strap Cyrus to his chest, the baby watching them curiously the entire time.

A short time later, they were all mounted and on their way. Fire held the spare Oryx's reins in one hand and wrapped his other arm around Quigley's waist. He cooed and chattered to Cyrus and the Oryx as they made their way closer to the Burnished Chieftain's city.

HOURS LATER, THEY STOPPED TO MAKE CAMP. DAVID AND Aster worked to make their campfire and Gram started dinner. Fire helped him unload the Oryx and tether them a short distance away from the camp.

Fire's nose wrinkled. "Baby boy needs a diaper change."

Quigley chuckled. "Hand him here, and I'll take care of it."

"I can do it," Fire said, bottom lip pushed out. "I'll be a good daddy."

"I know you will," Quigley agreed. "If you don't mind changing him, I'll keep setting up camp."

Fire grinned. "I got this."

Quigley left him to it, laughing aloud when he heard Fire gag when he took Cyrus's diaper off. Sara's son was a stinky one.

His smile faded as he thought of Sara. They hadn't had time to mourn her as they focused on making it to Star's Oasis, but that was often how life worked. *Gods, I hope you're at peace with Helara, Sara.*

After a dinner of rabbit and rice, they gathered around the campfire. Quigley leaned against his packs, David and Aster cuddled against his sides, while Gram fed Cyrus. Fire stood in front of them.

"Tell us your story, please," David said, eyes focused on Fire. "I wanna know where you come from."

Fire grinned. "A long, long time ago, I was just a little fire racing around my home world, Genarg. The planet was really nice to me, and I remember it whispering to me. It told me the best places to run and play."

Quigley stared at Fire. This had not been how he pictured Fire's story beginning.

Fire's voice turned wistful. "I spent a long time that way. Sometimes I miss it, but it was really lonely."

"You didn't have anyone to play with," David said, nodding in agreement. "I would have been lonely too."

"Eventually, the people on Genarg started making villages, then towns, then cities." Fire scowled. "They were the Crells, and they were really loud and fought a lot. I hated it."

"Did you talk to them?" Aster asked, hands reaching toward the warmth of the campfire. Desert nights were cold.

Fire wrinkled his nose. "No. They always got scared when I came close." His expression turned contemplative. "Then the planet talked to some of them and taught them how to see the spirit world around them. Those were the Crellic shamans."

"What do you mean they could see the spirit world?" Aster asked, leaning toward Fire.

Fire tapped his chin. "All around us is a thin layer that separates us from the spirit world. It's a place that shows the spiritual connection between everything. I can see it when I try, but I can't touch the threads connecting everything."

"Threads," Aster whispered, frowning. "Everything is connected."

Fire crouched down. "Yeah. Like when I look, I can see the connections between all of you." He frowned. "Wait, you didn't make our babies yourself?"

Quigley gave him a shocked look. "You can see that? David and Aster are my adopted children."

"They're still our babies," Fire said, nodding firmly. "The connection between you all is strong and solid. It doesn't matter that you didn't help make them. You love them and they love you."

"You're saying the Crellic shamans could see this world?" Gram asked, patting Cyrus's back as the baby burped loudly.

Fire smiled again and nodded. "Yep. Genarg helped them learn to see it and trained them to use that gift to help the Crells. They could touch and manipulate the connections to the world around them. Some could wield fire like me or make the rain fall or even make plants grow."

"How did that work out?" Quigley asked. "I can't imagine the clans with that kind of power."

Fire gave him a sad look. "Genarg was so sad when the shamans made the fighting worse. They were selfish and only cared about their own villages. They used their gifts to hurt others."

David sniffled. "You had to watch it all happen?"

Fire nodded, his own lip trembling. "I wanted to help, but I didn't know how." He turned his face up to the stars. "Then *she* came."

"Who?" Gram asked, looking as fascinated as the rest of them.

"My Queen," Fire whispered. "She had a name of her own, but she will always be my Queen when I remember her. She was a shaman and wanted the Crells to stop fighting and the world to be at peace. She worked with her most trusted shamans and created a ritual to summon the elements to fight beside her and unite the Crells."

"That's how you got a body?" David asked, looking him over. "You don't look that old."

Fire grinned. "This isn't my first body. When she did the ritual, I heard her call and answered. I wanted to help. Six Crells sacrificed their own lives to give the Queen's elements forms. The soul in my first body even said goodbye to me before he left. That body was big and green. I had long black hair and short tusks."

"Whoa," David said, eyes wide. "What did your feet look like?"

"They were huge," Fire said excitedly. "I didn't even have to wear shoes because the bottom of my feet were rough. I loved that body."

Quigley chuckled at Fire's expression of joy.

"Was the Queen able to save the Crells?" Aster asked, bringing them back into the story.

Fire nodded. "We did it. We united the Crells, and after the fighting ended, she led them peacefully. We lived out that cycle protecting the Crells and squashing any fighting before it started."

"We?" Gram asked, tilting her head. "You weren't the only element?"

"Nope. There were five others. This cycle we call them Water, Air, Life, Earth, and Death. Earth and Death are my friends, but the others were always jerks." Fire narrowed his eyes. "They liked hurting people."

"Were they really mean?" Aster asked.

Fire nodded furiously. "Death always had to go and stomp Water, Air, and Life's butts. He kept them in line."

"What happened when your body grew old?" David asked.

"It died," Fire said, shrugging. "I went back to being a flame. Genarg was happy with me too."

"How did you end up here in this body, then?" Quigley asked. "Not that I'm complaining. I have my mate, and you're the most amazing being I've ever met."

Fire preened. "Thank you, love muffin."

Gram snorted and the kids giggled.

Quigley winced. "Love muffin?"

Fire nodded. "That's your pet name. Sebby and Alois have pet names too. It's what mates do."

Gram laughed hard. "He has you there, love muffin. You'll have to deal with it."

"Anyway," Fire said, standing back up. "The Crells didn't stay peaceful after our cycles ended. They remembered the power of my Queen though. A long time after our bodies died, they summoned us again. They messed it up though. The Queen's soul was brought back, but it was corrupted."

Fire gave Quigley a distressed look, then ran to him and climbed in his lap.

Quigley and the others hugged him, and Fire seemed to settle down a bit.

"Was it bad?" David asked.

Fire shivered. "It was really bad. She wasn't my Queen anymore. She was a monster and made me do things. Horrible things. Eventually, the Crells would manage to kill us, but generations later, they'd bring us back, and it would happen all over again."

"I'm so sorry," Quigley said, kissing the side of his head. "I wish you never had to suffer such things."

Fire swallowed hard and nodded. "The Crells killed themselves fighting. This last time we were brought back by others. The Queen tried to destroy the whole galaxy, but we stopped her. Death and Sebby saved me from her, and we fought back. Now, her soul is her own again, and we'll never be summoned to kill people. Not ever."

"Good," Quigley managed to say. He hugged Fire and the kids tightly. "Now you can just live."

"With you," Fire said, placing a soft kiss on his chin. "My mate."

CHAPTER 5

*F*ire listened to David and Gram's loud snores. *They're worse than Mordy*, he thought with a grin. He lay with Quigley a distance from the campfire, but he could still hear them. How Cyrus was managing to sleep between the two was a mystery. Aster was the only graceful sleeper.

He rolled his head on Quigley's arm and stared at his mate's profile.

Quigley's lips twitched. "Go to sleep."

"Why can't we have sex?" he whispered.

"I don't want the kids to be traumatized," Quigley said, chuckling. "We don't have the tent set up, so we have no privacy. Is it so hard to wait?"

Fire sighed. "I guess not. It's just I never got to have sex before. I wasn't interested during my first cycle and was too busy trying to resist the Queen's control in all my others. This is the first time I've ever even wanted to try it."

His mate's muscular body was *right* there too. Fire didn't understand how people possibly resisted their mates.

"Why haven't you tried it?" Quigley asked, giving him a

curious look. "You said you've lived in peace at Charybdis for a few years now."

"Charybdis Station," Fire corrected and pointed up at the sky. "It's somewhere up there. It's not supposed to be a planet, but it feels like one. It talks to me like Genarg did."

Quigley whistled softly. "People built a planet? That's beyond amazing."

Fire nodded. "They're really good people too. I love them."

"You didn't want any of them?" Quigley asked. "Not that it's a bad thing if you didn't. One thing I've noticed over the years is that every person is different in what they need. I managed to find a few men when my clan would meet with other clans, and it offered some comfort. If I was attracted to women, it would have been easier."

Fire made a face. He didn't like thinking about his mate with other people. "I tried to want people, but I only wanted a few people like that and they were my friends, so it didn't seem right to try and sex them up."

"'Sex them up'?" Quigley asked, voice full of amusement.

Fire nodded. "I didn't let them see all my glorious sexiness, but don't worry. You'll get to see it all. I have really pretty underwear back on the ship. I got them from my friend Finn. He tried to teach me aerial silk dancing, but I set his favorite silk on fire, so he just gives me pretty underwear now."

Quigley cleared his throat and shifted under the blanket. "I didn't know underwear could be pretty."

"You'll see," Fire said, patting his chest. "Anyway, my dick kinda liked my friends Shae, Juniper, and Donnal. Not as much as it likes you though."

"This may be the strangest conversation I've ever had,"

Quigley said, "and I've had some really weird ones with my sister."

Fire paused at the pain that filled his mate's voice when he said 'sister.' "Quigley? What happened to her? She should be here with Cyrus."

Quigley sighed. "Sara was a surprise to Mom and Dad when she came along. She was ten years younger than me. A couple of years after she was born, Mom and Dad died while out on a hunt. Gram and Grandpa took us in, but I did my best to raise Sara so they could focus on keeping us alive."

"I'm sorry," Fire whispered, eyes watering. He hated the pain he felt in his mate. So much pain.

"Our clan isn't a very good one." Quigley pulled Fire closer and ran a hand down his back. "There are certain things they don't like. They only wanted us to read and speak the old language, the one the Burnished used before offworld settlers came to our planet. The clan elders wanted us to be strong and hard hearted. Anything not of our world or even anything simply different wasn't allowed."

"That's stupid," Fire said, scowling.

"Grandpa taught us all the common language." Quigley waved toward his face. "You can hear that though. All the clans speak it, but ours was trying to stomp it out."

"Sebastian calls it Galactic," Fire said, nuzzling against Quigley's neck. "Sebby is really smart and knows all kinds of languages."

"I wish I did. The clan elder would have killed us if they overheard us speaking *Galactic,* even though most of us learned at least bits and pieces of it." Quigley leaned back a little and pulled the blanket down. "There were reasons my family didn't want to draw attention to itself."

Fire watched with wide eyes as Quigley pulled his long tunic up. The moonlight shone brightly on his muscled stomach and chest. It took a moment for Fire to notice the Wello dots mixed in among Quigley's markings.

Fire slid a hand over the long, thin, barely there line dissecting Quigley's abdomen. "You have Wello blood. You can have babies."

"Maybe," Quigley said. "I don't know. Grandpa said that some with the birthing line can and some can't. Either way, the clan never let anyone born with a birthing line live."

Fire scowled. "I don't like them."

"Me neither," Quigley said, releasing a heavy breath. He pulled the blanket back up and over his chest. "We hid it from my dad since he was very traditional. When Sara had Cyrus, I was there. His line is a lot like mine and half hidden by markings. The clan found out. When Sara ran away from the clan to meet us, they chased her. She gave me Cyrus and stayed to hold them off."

"That's what you were going to do." Fire wiped at his tears. "You were going to die for them."

"That's what she did," Quigley said quietly. "I just wanted to keep them safe. They would kill all of them, not just Cyrus and me."

"I won't let them hurt you," Fire said. "I'll be like Fluffle and protect my family."

"You've already saved my life," Quigley said, smiling. "We're survivors. If given half a chance, we'll be just fine."

"I want you to be more than *fine*," Fire said, sniffing. "You have to be happy too."

Quigley kissed the side of his head again, and Fire huffed. He wanted a real kiss.

"By the way, who is Fluffle?"

Fire smiled wide. "The fiercest being in all the galaxy. The only one who comes close to him is his person, Selene. Together, they're unstoppable."

"Hmm, I hear a little hero worship in your voice." Quigley chuckled.

"Who was your hero?" Fire asked, yawning. The long day was starting to catch up to him.

"That's easy. Gram and Grandpa. They taught Sara and I how to survive, but they also taught us how to love. They were true mates and honored one another. I thought Gram would die when we lost Grandpa, but she pushed through for me and the kids."

"Do you miss him?" Fire asked, sad. He wished Gram still had her mate and Quigley his grandpa.

"Every day. He liked to tell us the stories of our gods." Quigley pointed up at the smaller, gold moon hanging in the sky. "Have you ever heard the story of Helara?"

"Nope." Fire snuggled in close. His mate was the best snuggler ever. Even better than Mordy, though Fire would never tell the baby so.

"Gram told us the story when we were kids. Long before the offworlders came, long before our traditions were founded, there was the first clan, Braxia, home of the Burnished gods. Each god had their place in the clan. Some were protectors, some were hunters, some were nurturers. While each of them had a purpose and were honored, they fought among each other. Maybe they wanted more recognition or a higher rank in the clan. Whatever the case, there was plenty of petty backstabbing and machinations. Despite this, all of them, every last one, honored and respected one god, Helara. They called him the heart of the clan."

"Why?" Fire asked, blinking sleepily.

"Helara was joy, love, and peace, all in one. He comforted the gods when they were sad, eased their anger when they lost their tempers, and took them to task when they did something foolish. He kept the clan strong, yes, but he also protected the Burnished. There were many gods who wanted to torment the mortals. They took great joy in torturing them with their tricks, but Helara always stepped in and said *enough* when it got too bad."

Quigley paused and pulled the covers closer around Fire as a light wind blew through.

"One day, Helara was disguised and walking among the Burnished. He watched them argue with each other and fight. He saw their pettiness and cruelty and grew sad. They acted just like the gods that tormented them."

"What did he do?" Fire asked, frowning. He would have sent Fluffle to deal with them if he was Helara.

"He stepped in to protect a Burnished that was being beaten." Quigley was quiet for a moment. "The other Burnished turned on him. They tore at his body and tried to kill him."

"No," Fire whispered, eyes widening. "Not Helara."

Quigley nodded. "The gods were enraged and came to the mortals. They killed many and scorched the entire planet."

"What about Helara?" Fire smoothed a hand across Quigley's chest, enjoying the steady beat of his heart.

"Helara tried to stop them. He gave each Burnished an inner flame so they could protect themselves. The gods didn't understand why he would do that. They turned their anger on him, and their attack was far worse than the mortals' had been."

Quigley held his hand up, the markings on his skin heated and turned a golden red. A small flame sprouted from his palm.

Fire blew and the flame grew higher. He ran his fingers through the tiny blaze. It felt like Quigley, and Fire loved it.

Quigley slowly closed his hand and the flame snuffed out.

"What did they do to Helara?" Fire asked, hugging tightly to Quigley.

"They broke his bones and shed his blood all across the planet. As he lay bleeding, they realized what they had done and begged his forgiveness."

"Did he forgive them?" Fire wouldn't have. He would have run far away.

Quigley shook his head. "He gave up on them. Helara said he was done protecting the cruel, be they god or mortal. The earth beneath him wept as it healed him and helped him stand. Helara left Braxia for good and refused to ever see any of the other gods again."

"What about the innocent ones?" Fire asked, looking up at the golden shining moon.

"Gram said that Helara brings the abandoned and unloved to live with him there," Quigley said, pointing up at the moon. "He loves them and cares for them."

Fire had seen the moon up close. It was a ball of gas and rock. "Do you believe it?"

Quigley sighed. "No. I don't think the moon holds all our abandoned and unloved. I hope though. I hope that somewhere, maybe in your spirit world, Helara does watch over them."

"I hope so too," Fire said, hugging him.

"Grandpa spoke a lot about Helara. He said it was important to remember why love is essential to the world. It doesn't make us weak or foolish. Instead it gives us hope and something to believe in."

Fire leaned over Quigley. "I think I would have liked your grandpa."

Quigley grinned. "He would have been telling me to put the damn tent up and admire your sexiness."

Fire's laugh froze on his lips when Quigley pulled him

down for a kiss. His mate's lips were warm and a little rough on his own. When Quigley's tongue swiped across Fire's lips, heat curled through him, setting him ablaze in a far different way than he was used to.

He rolled on top of Quigley and arched his hips against his mate. Quigley's arms pulled him close, and he rolled Fire beneath him before breaking the kiss.

Quigley's dark eyes watched him from above. Fire felt his hard length pressing into his stomach. "Good night."

Fire blinked, confused. "What?"

"Sleep well, Fire." Quigley pulled his hips away and arranged them beneath the blanket again.

Fire's heartbeat gradually slowed. "No sex?"

Quigley chuckled and pulled him against his chest. "No sex."

"Thank the gods," Aster said, voice full of disgust.

FIRE WOKE UP BEFORE SUNRISE THE NEXT MORNING. HE TOOK a moment to watch his mate sleep. Quigley was fast becoming an obsession. There were so many facets to him that Fire wanted to explore. He was a hard-faced hunter, a doting father, a sweet romantic.

Quigley was a puzzle that Fire would enjoy unraveling.

He reluctantly left their blankets and checked on the rest of the family. David and Aster were both still sleeping soundly, but Gram was awake.

She blinked at him sleepily as she slowly sat up. "Usually I'm the first one up."

"What can I do to help?" he asked softly, eyes moving to check on Cyrus. The baby was starting to stir, and it looked like his diaper was wet.

Gram patted his back. "Why don't you take care of Cyrus there while I get started on breakfast. These three always wake up starving."

"I like babies," Fire said, picking up Cyrus and cuddling his close. "You need a clean diaper and some milk, baby boy."

Cyrus cooed and tugged on his toes while Fire deftly changed his diaper. He wished he had some of the powder that Sebastian used for Mordy. He dug through the bags and found a long, wide scarf. It was covering a pile of phasors.

"Gram, do you know how to use a phasor?" he asked over his shoulder.

"Sure do," she said proudly. "Those were my mate's. He brought them from his clan and taught me how to use them. We taught the kids too. The clan elder never much liked it, but they're commonly used in other clans. My mate knew a man in Star's Oasis that could repair them too."

"I wasn't expecting that," Fire said, pulling the scarf around him and Cyrus. "Surprises all day long, Cy. Poop it. This isn't working."

Fire spent the next ten minutes trying to figure out how to tie Cyrus to him like Sebastian did with Mordy.

Aster yawned and knelt beside him. "What are you doing? You're making a lot of noise for someone who is just changing a diaper."

"I want Cy to be closer to me than his bag thing will let him." Fire groaned. "Sebby makes this look easy."

Aster giggled. "I can help. The women in the encampment use these to carry the babies as they work. This was Aunt Sara's."

Fire stayed still and let Aster quickly wrap the scarf around him and Cyrus. "Do you miss her?"

Aster nodded. "She lived with us until she married last

year. It's hard to imagine her gone. Sometimes my mind tells me I'll feel her over the next sand dune, but then she's not there. For Dad, I think it's worse."

Fire looked over his shoulder. Their blankets were empty and already rolled up. *I need to find my mate.*

"Dad always goes to watch the sunrise." Aster tied an intricate knot, then stood. "I'm glad you're here, Fire. Dad needs you."

Fire stood and hugged the girl, squeezing her until she laughed and hugged him back. "It's okay to miss your aunt, Aster. It's okay to be sad. Sometimes that's what our hearts need to heal."

She hugged him tighter. "I don't like thinking about it."

Fire swung her around a little, being careful not to squash Cyrus. "That's alright. Think about Charybdis Station then. We're gonna have fun, okay? I'll show you all the good napping spots in the neighborhood, and we'll get you a kitten. That's what good parents do. I'll be a good dad."

She giggled as he swung her around the camp and set her down next to Gram.

Gram shook her head. She already had bread and fruit ready for breakfast. "You two are silly things. Aren't they, David?"

David paused his talk with the goat to look at them. "Yeah. They're strange, but we love them anyway."

Fire's stomach growled, and he eyed the small ration of food. He couldn't wait to get back to Juniper. His friend was a wonderful cook and always had something yummy ready for Fire to eat.

"Don't you eye our food that way," Gram said, smacking his arm. "We eat what we can when traveling. This is actually a very good breakfast compared to what we normally have."

"When we get to Charybdis Station, I'm gonna feed you

all so much food you pop." Fire rubbed Cyrus's back. "Even Cyrus."

"Will they let us live on Charybdis Station?" Gram asked, voice doubtful. "That's up in the sky, and we've never been on one of those flying ships. We've seen them sometimes, in the sky, but we've never been on one."

"Of course you can come home with me," Fire said, sniffing. "They love me, and that means they'll love you too."

The sun was slowly rising, so Fire hurried off to find his mate. He didn't want Quigley to be alone if he was sad.

He found him kneeling in the sand, face raised toward the sun. Quigley had a bow hooked around him, so Fire couldn't cuddle with him, but he could still hold his hand.

Fire plopped into the sand and grabbed Quigley's hand in both of his.

Quigley's lips twitched, and he adjusted his bow before pulling Fire into his side.

They stayed quiet as the sun rose higher. *It's pretty here,* he thought, a little sad that they would be leaving the planet. *If I'm sad, then Quig has to be even sadder.*

"I should have asked you." Fire kept his voice soft. "Do you want to move to Charybdis Station with me?"

He didn't want to even contemplate leaving Sebastian and the others, but Quigley was his mate.

"I do," Quigley said, voice rough. "I love the desert, but the clans aren't safe for us. Dustin will keep coming, and he'll bring every warrior he can with him."

"I can protect us," Fire said, tilting his chin up. "I've been in a lot of battles."

"You hated fighting," Quigley reminded him. "I won't ask you to do that. I want you to live happy and free, not be tied to the violence that you spent so long running from."

Fire sighed, happiness and the sun warming him inside

and out. "You're a good mate, and I'll try hard to— Look! What's that?"

Fire wiggled away from Quigley and ran quickly to the closest rock. He knelt and looked beneath it. A small black lizard stared back at him with luminous dark eyes. Its tongue darted out and licked its snout.

"Hi," Fire said, reaching his hand out. "I'm Fire. You're really pretty, and I think we should be friends."

The lizard tilted his head and watched Fire carefully. His mind brushed against Fire's, making him shiver.

"That's a venomous black stinger," Quigley said, pulling him away from the rock. "They're deadly."

"He seems scared," Fire said, kneeling back down. "I won't hurt you."

The lizard watched him steadily and sent Fire the image of a large bird of prey swooping down to grab another lizard.

Fire whimpered. "Quig, his friend got eaten by a hawk, and Cinnamon's scared. We need to help him."

Quigley tried pulling him up again. "The stinger doesn't need our help, Fire. Trust me."

"He says he does," Fire said, sticking his tongue out at Quigley. "His name is Cinnamon, and he's my friend."

"Helara save me," Quigley groaned. "Fine. We'll see if we can get it to a larger rock. It'll find food there."

Fire watched as Quigley set his bow down in the sand and slid it under the rock.

Cinnamon gave Fire a curious look, and Fire shrugged. "I think he wants you to get on the bow."

Cinnamon ran up the bow and over Quigley's arm to rest on his shoulder.

Quigley froze, eyes widening in panic. "Fire, run. Get Cyrus away. I'll need to burn it off."

Fire rolled his eyes and picked Cinnamon up, settling him on his own shoulder. "Cinnamon thinks you're ridiculous."

Cinnamon shook his head. *Didn't think that.*

"Shh," Fire whispered. "We gotta show him that you're not dangerous."

Quigley grabbed his hand and pulled him closer, eyes focused on Cinnamon. "Fire, can you talk to animals?"

"Sometimes," Fire said, smiling. "When they're my friends."

"Cinnamon is a friend?" Quigley asked. "He's less than a foot away from Cyrus, Fire."

Cinnamon hissed, not liking the implication that he would hurt the baby.

"Cinnamon is my friend," Fire said. "Sometimes, that's what happens. Those threads I told you about last night, the ones that connect all of us?"

Quigley nodded.

"Sometimes they show us who we need to be connected to. Cinnamon and me are friends. He won't hurt our babies. I promise."

Quigley released a long breath. "You're going to turn my hair gray, mate. I'll look older than Gram within the year."

Fire giggled and rubbed a hand over Cyrus's head. "He's silly, Cy, isn't he? He really needs to learn how to make friends."

"Dad," David yelled out as he ran toward them. "Look over there!"

They turned around and faced toward the east. A shuttle flew toward them, and Fire recognized the insignia of The Blue Solace.

"Hey, I know that shuttle," Fire said, running toward David and the rest of the camp. "Come meet Cinnamon before they land. Don't tell them he's venomous, okay? They'll be all weird like your dad."

David watched Cinnamon with wide eyes. "You're the best thing to ever happen to us, Fire. I want a black stinger too, Dad."

"No," Quigley said, ruffling David's hair. "You have a goat. Deal with it."

The shuttle landed not far from them, and the door opened immediately. Fire recognized Alois running toward them. Jellybean rode on his friend's shoulder, and Alois's dog, Perri, ran at his side.

Fire was vaguely aware of his mate and the others staring at Alois in shock. Sebastian's mate was a Dedril and had red scales framing his face. Fire kept forgetting that his new family had never seen other species before.

"You are in so much trouble, Fire." Alois handed Fire his Gueina pig and pulled him into a hug. "Sebastian is worried sick about you. He told you to be back by nightfall. I was there and heard him say it. He sent me looking in this direction, convinced you had been captured by desert pirates or something."

Missed you, Jellybean thought, squeaking at him aloud.

Fire cuddled Jellybean to his chest and hugged Alois back. "Sorry, guys. I got distracted in a really good way." A throat cleared behind him, and Fire pushed Alois back and turned to wave at Quigley and the others. "Everyone, this is Alois and Jellybean."

Alois looked them over, eyes softening at the sight of the children.

Fire kissed Jellybean's head. "Alois and Jellybean, this is my mate, Quig. Isn't he the most handsome being you've ever seen? He's all mine too. Mine."

Quigley's dark skin flushed a deep red and Gram snickered.

Jellybean squeaked and wiggled his legs, wanted to be put down. Fire settled him in the sand, and his friend ran as fast as he could to Quigley. Fire's mate eyed the guinea pig before stooping to pick him up.

I like him, Jellybean said, scrambling to sit on Quigley's shoulder and sniff his ear.

"I'm glad, Jellybean. He needs lots of love." Fire smiled proudly and pointed out the others. "I also have a Gram and three babies. Three, Alois. This is Cyrus, David, and Aster. Oh, and this is my friend Cinnamon. He's not deadly at all."

CHAPTER 6

Quigley's stomach lurched as the shuttle dipped down as they approached Star's Oasis, making him wish they hadn't taken the time to eat breakfast before loading everyone on the shuttle. David and his goat stood with Fire, watching the city approach. Quigley didn't understand how his son could look so excited as the ship moved.

"What's it look like, Dad?" Aster asked. "It feels different from when we were here last time."

The clan had stopped coming to Star's Oasis when the new chieftain had taken control. Before then, the city had been very similar to their encampment, only with stone houses instead of tents.

Quigley cursed his stomach and looked out of the window. "There are many more houses than before. I see more animal pens and crop fields too. There are shuttles like this one flying around the city, but there are even larger ships. Some are bigger than our whole encampment."

Alois briefly looked over his shoulder from where he sat up front with Perri. "On the other side of the city are new irrigation fields. A few of the planets in the system have helped Chieftain Bowan increase agricultural production. The ships you see are mostly trading vessels. Burnished Outpost has access to unique minerals, so they've been making a place for themselves in our system."

Quigley shook his head. "Our clan knew nothing of this. Once Chieftain Bowan took control, the clan elder refused to come to Star's Oasis. We stayed deeper in the desert and did without the yearly trading."

"Is the marketplace still there?" Aster asked, voice hopeful.

Quigley quickly looked down and up. "It's there."

Gram chuckled. "Having trouble, Quig?"

Fire spun around and came to him, climbing on his lap. "Are you alright? Do you not like the shuttle? It takes getting used to if you're not familiar with it. Here, hold Jellybean. He always makes me feel better."

Quigley let Fire settle the small, furry rodent in his hands. The creature's chubby cheeks moved as he squeaked. "Thank you, Jellybean."

Alois snorted and started to lower the shuttle. "You two are something else."

Fire hummed under his breath and moved Cinnamon to sit on Quigley's shoulder.

"You're certain the black stinger won't kill me?" Quigley asked, voice soft. He was much more comfortable holding the rodent than he was the lizard.

"He promises he'll be good." Fire kissed him. "He's part of the family now."

Quigley nodded, mind dazed from the taste of Fire on his lips. "That's good then."

Gram chuckled. "I believe you're right, Alois. Those two are something alright."

Quigley ignored them and pulled Fire closer. Cyrus still rode happily in the baby sling and didn't seem to mind being squashed between them.

"Will I be able to speak to your clan elder soon?" Quigley whispered.

Fire nodded and pet Cinnamon's head. "They'll want to meet you when we get home."

Quigley nodded. He wanted Fire's leaders to accept Quigley and his family. Fire seemed certain they would, but Quigley knew that leaders had to consider all aspects of a situation before making a decision. They may love Fire, but taking in five more people was asking a lot.

The shuttle finally landed, and Quigley sighed in relief. The constant vibration running through his bones stilled and his gut settled.

Alois unstrapped himself and stood. "I'll make sure your Oryx and packs are taken care of. You'll stay with the rest of us in the chieftain's home."

"Really?" David asked, mouth hanging open.

Alois passed him and ruffled his hair. "Absolutely."

The back of the shuttle opened up, startling Quigley. The Oryx shuffled their feet and bleated nervously. He stood and set Fire back on his feet just as someone pushed into the already crowded shuttle.

"Why are there Oryx in my shuttle?" a man asked. He was Burnished, like Quigley, but dressed very differently than any Burnished Quigley had ever seen.

"Sorry, Hack," Alois said, grinning unapologetically. "Fire made some friends, and these critters came with them.

"Fire?" A man pushed past Hack. "You had better have a good explanation, young man. You were supposed to be back by sunset, and I felt you use a lot of your power yesterday."

Fire ran to the man and hugged him. "Sebby, I met my

mate! My dick really likes him too, but so does my heart. I just want to hold him forever."

Quigley flushed at Fire's words while the others laughed.

Well, all except the man hugging Fire. As Quigley looked Sebastian over, he grew distinctly uncomfortable. The man was much younger than he had pictured from Fire's stories. He looked to be only a few years older than Fire. Well, Fire's body.

Sebastian met his gaze, eyes narrowed. "You're Fire's mate?"

Quigley glared back, letting his inner fire fill his eyes. "Yes, I am. You should release him. Now."

Sebastian growled and pushed Fire to the side. "Don't you dare tell me what to do. Fire is mine to protect, and I don't know a thing about you. If you think you can just walk in here and take him away from his family, I'm going to bury your big, burly ass in all that sand out there."

"Whoa, love," Alois said, coming to stand behind Sebastian. He settled his hands on his mate's shoulders. "Quigley isn't here to take Fire away from us. Fire is bringing Quig and his family into our family. We just got larger, not smaller."

"Sebby," Fire said, pouting. "You're supposed to love my mate and give him lots of hugs and food."

Quigley gave Sebastian a smug look. "You heard him."

Fire smacked his arm. "You're being mean too, Quig. You have to love Sebby."

Quigley scowled. "He shouldn't touch you."

"I'll touch him all I want," Sebastian said, voice rising. "He's my son."

Fire's eyes grew wide and he turned to Sebastian. "I am?"

"Did you really doubt it?" Alois asked, voice full of amusement. He turned to Quigley. "I know you're feeling protective of your mate, but Sebastian and I love Fire too. He's our son, despite him looking just a little younger than us. He's a special soul, and we've taken care of him since we met."

"It's *my* honor to care for him now," Quigley said, trying to keep the anger from his voice. "I'll try to be less..." He struggled to find the right word.

"Bossy, grumpy, and a pain in the ass," Gram filled in for him, chuckling.

Sebastian snorted. "Very good choice of words."

Gram settled her hand on Sebastian's arm. "Come on. I'll tell you all the embarrassing stories I have about my grandson. You can think on them when he gets all growly."

Sebastian smiled and took her hand. "I'm going to like you. I can already tell."

"That's my Gram," Fire said, bouncing from foot to foot. "I have three babies too. This is Cyrus. His mama died, so Quig and I are gonna raise him. Then, this is Aster, who is really smart and can sense the spirit word, and David, who loves animals like me. That's his friend Gracie."

Sebastian's mouth opened and closed, and Quigley could sense the conflict in him.

Alois grinned and nuzzled against his mate's neck. "We're going to need a bigger attic."

Sebastian's quick laugh turned into a sigh. "I wasn't ready for this."

"Parents never are," Gram said sadly. "My Quigley is a good man. He may be broodier than a hen, but he knows the value of loving family. We'll all make good additions to your clan."

Sebastian shook his head. "Of course you will. What am I thinking, making you stand here all day while I have a hissy fit." He smiled at Aster and David. "Please come with me, and I'll help you all get settled, then we'll go to the market. I've been itching to go since we landed."

Quigley started to follow, but Sebastian pressed a hand to his chest, stopping him. "Alois, take Quigley and show him around the shooting range."

Alois rolled his eyes. "Yes, dear."

Hack snickered. The man had been watching them from the side for a while. "I'll come too. We'll give Quigley here *the talk*."

Alois gave Hack a flat look. "*The talk* didn't work on Gravy. He still got my sweet, innocent Periwinkle pregnant."

Quigley looked at Perri. The fuzzy dog watched them, tongue hanging out. "Please tell me Gravy is a dog."

"Of course he is," Hack said, frowning.

"Sometimes I don't know for sure who's a pet and who isn't when Fire tells me about them," Quigley said, shrugging.

"That's because it doesn't matter," Fire said and gave Quigley a kiss on the cheek. "I'll buy you something nice at the market. Sebby, I need some credits."

Sebastian led them away, and Quigley groaned. "You forgot Jellybean and your death lizard."

Fire waved at him and kept going.

"Death lizard?" Hack arched a brow and eyed Cinnamon. "Is that a black stinger? Why is it on your shoulder?"

Quigley sighed and used one finger to pat the animal's head. "Fire made a friend."

A man with wine red hair ran into the shuttle and squealed at the sight of the Oryx. "What are these adorable donkey/goat/sheep things?"

Hack groaned. "You can't have one, Leti. They all belong to Quigley."

Quigley smirked. "Well, really just five of the Oryx belong to me."

Hack glared at him. "Let's go to the shooting range. I have the urge to blast someone in the head."

Quigley fought a laugh and noticed another man following behind Leti and holding a child. The baby was clearly burnished with golden skin and birth markings that looked like Hack's. His hair, though, was the same wine red of Hack's mate.

I wonder what my own child will look like. He pictured a miniature Fire running around and grinned.

The man carrying the child was young and delicate looking. His small stature and fine features would encourage many to dismiss him as a threat, but the way he watched Quigley identified him as a predator.

Alois patted Quigley's shoulder. "Quig, this is Leti, Hack's mate, and Wolfe, Leti's good friend and constant guard. He's holding Milo, Hack and Leti's youngest child. For now."

"Can I have this one?" Leti asked, hugging one of the spare Oryx Quigley had collected after Sara's death. "Please?"

Quigley smiled. "She's yours."

Hack groaned and gave Leti a kiss. "What's one more pet, right? I'm taking Quigley to the shooting range to use him as target practice. I'll be back by dinner."

Leti patted his new pet's nose. "You have one hour. You're supposed to spend time with your younger siblings, but every time they come close, you run. They don't hate you, Will."

Hack grabbed Quigley's arm and tugged him away. "Sorry, love. I have to go scare Fire's mate. I'll try to be back soon."

Leti rolled his eyes and focused on the Oryx.

Wolfe watched them leave, eyes narrowed on Quigley. *Another friend of Fire's*, Quigley thought with a sigh.

He turned and gave Hack a curious look. "Why is your mate unhappy with you?"

Hack winced. "I wasn't raised on Burnished Outpost."

"How is that possible?" Quigley asked, surprised. "You're Burnished."

"My mother left me in the deep desert," Hack said, eyes hard. "I was just a kid."

Quigley sighed. "I'm sorry to hear that. My clan elder wanted to abandon Gram, David, and Aster too, but I refused. How did you survive?"

Hack's face softened. "Charybdis Station sends training patrols to fly over the deep desert every few days. My adopted dad found me and took me in. When Bowan took over as chieftain, we found out I had younger siblings. A few came to live with me, but the youngest stayed with Bowan."

"You feel guilty for not insisting they come to you?" Quigley guessed.

Alois snorted. "Really, Hack?"

Hack flushed. "I can't help it. They seem happy here with Bowan, but I'm their brother. I should have taken them in."

"Bowan is their uncle," Alois said. "He's family too."

"Enough," Hack said, pulling Quigley to a stop. "We're here."

Quigley looked around. The shooting range was full of offworld soldiers. He took a moment to study the different species and tried to put a name to them. The large, furry beings were Grell, and the ones with horns were Sirens. He knew that much from Grandpa's stories.

"Selene," Hack yelled, waving his arm. "This is Fire's *mate*."

A tall Siren with curled horns and black hair, turned to stare at him. Her face remained impassive, but her eyes were full of curiosity. "He has a bow and arrows," she said, voice monotone.

"Phasors aren't as useful when you can shoot flames," Hack said, summoning a bit of his inner fire to dance around his hand. "A bow is a good hunting weapon."

Quigley moved to stand in front of the woman. "I can fire a phasor as well. My grandpa trained me. I prefer the bow for hunting, but I'm also a good warrior."

Selene nodded. "Let's see."

A nearby offworlder whooped loudly. "Selene's about to kick a new guy's ass. My money's on Selene, of course."

Alois winced. "I'll bet on Quigley. He's family, damn it."

A small crowd gathered around them, but Quigley ignored them to study his opponent. Selene moved gracefully, but there was power within her slender form. He knew a predator when he saw one.

"Go easy on him, Selene," Hack said, patting Quigley's shoulder. "We don't want to hurt him too much. Fire will be upset."

"I love Fire," Selene said, voice flat and emotionless. "You will treat him well."

Quigley nodded and unhooked his bow from his back. He would have to take her by surprise – though with the way she assessed him, that would be hard. "I will."

Selene drew a long, strange-looking blade from behind her. "We start now."

Quigley barely saw her move and darted to the side. He pulled his bow out slightly, and she tripped, stumbling briefly.

That was enough time for Quigley to quickly fire an arrow.

Selene paused, looking over her shoulder. Her long braid was pinned to one of the many posts holding the canvas tent above the shooting range.

The crowd around them was completely silent as they all stared at the arrow.

Selene's face stayed expressionless, but Quigley saw the excitement in her eyes. "Draif?"

One of the men in the crowd grinned. "You rushed, Selene. You were expecting his skill, but underestimated the bow."

She reached back and pulled the arrow from her braid. "Again."

"I'm next." A large man with feline ears and sharp fangs gave him a hard look. "Fire's my friend, and we need to make sure you're worthy of him."

"I'm after Lucas," another man said.

Alois held his hands up. "Okay, now. You'll all get a turn, but make sure you don't hurt him too bad. Fire really likes him."

LATER THAT NIGHT, QUIGLEY SHIFTED IN HIS CHAIR ON THE balcony of his own room. His body ached from the hours of sparring Selene and her friends had put him through. Alois and Hack had sat back, feet up and drinks in hand, as he endured the most intense workout of his life. *Bastards*.

Quigley stared out over the city of Star's Oasis. He had never been inside one of the large houses, and the chieftain's home was truly a palace.

The city was so different than the last time he had seen it. Offworlder technology mixed with Burnished Outpost's traditional architecture. Even the market had grown.

He smoothed a hand over the beautiful gold and amber ear cuff Fire had brought him. Quigley had never owned something so beautiful before. Ear adornments weren't considered appropriate for a hunter, but Quigley loved it.

He had felt a little less special when he saw the jeweled harness Fire and David had picked out for Gracie. The goat had pranced around, practically preening.

Quigley also didn't particularly love the kitten Fire had bought Aster. The little beast was a white, fluffy ball of hate. At least when Quigley was around. Sebastian had loved it.

"What's wrong?" Fire asked, rocking Cyrus to sleep in his arms. He sat in another chair across from Quigley. "Did Hack and Alois scare you?"

"I like them," Quigley admitted with a smile, shifting in his seat again. "It's just very odd to be here. We're going to have dinner with the chieftain."

"Bowan is nice," Fire said, yawning. "He said I could come run in the deserts anytime, but I couldn't leave my fire wall burning."

"Bowan," Quigley repeated, shaking his head. "He lets us call him Bowan, and his mate is a man and is pregnant with his second child. I never thought something like that would happen or that I'd be somewhere like this."

Fire cooed at Cyrus and settled the baby into his bassinet.

Cinnamon curled on top of the basket, sleeping, and Jellybean snuggled beside Cyrus once he settled down. Quigley smiled, wishing he had had a Jellybean and Cinnamon when he was a child. He and David were far too much alike.

Fire petted Jellybean's brown and white furry back, then sat on Quigley's lap. "Changes are scary, aren't they?"

Quigley frowned. "I'm not scared."

"I get scared sometimes." Fire settled his head on

Quigley's shoulder. "Every time Sebastian takes a new apprentice, I'm afraid he'll get tired of me and make me leave."

Quigley snorted. "That's never going to happen. He loves you."

"I know that here," Fire said, tapping his head, "but it's hard to remember it here," he finished, patting his chest. "Before Sebastian, I was alone. My queen wasn't really my queen anymore, and Death was too busy trying to survive. Then Sebby saved me and loved me. He's my family, just like you, Gram, and the kids are. I don't want to lose that. Not ever."

Quigley stroked his mate's back. "You'll never be alone again, Fire. Between Sebastian and me, you'll always have a family."

Fire snuggled against him. "You will too. No matter how much things change over the next few months, I'll always be right here with you."

Quigley's arms tightened around his mate. The sands may be shifting under his feet, but Fire was right. There were constants in his life. His mate and his family.

CHAPTER 7

Fire stole another piece of fruit from Quigley's plate and stuffed it in his mouth. The food on Burnished Outpost was different than what he was used to, but it was good. He especially liked the Gaora cactus fruit.

"You'll train with me starting tomorrow, Quigley," Selene said. She sat with her mate and son across from them. "You need to learn our technology, but I have some ideas for your bow. We'll be on Burnished Outpost for three more weeks, so that gives us a head start."

"I appreciate it," Quigley said, nodding.

Fire squeezed his mate's thigh under the table, making him wince. "You sure you don't need to rest up from today?"

Quigley snuggled Cyrus closer and glared at Fire. "I'm alright."

Fire sighed. "Mates are so stubborn."

"I know, right?" Leti gave Hack a look. "They should just listen to their husbands and do as they're told."

Hack gave his mate a stubborn look, then smiled tentatively at one of his younger brothers, Darrin.

The boy smiled back. "We won't bite, Will. Laurie won't let us."

Laurie, Bowan's mate, rolled his eyes. "Like that's ever stopped you from doing something."

Fire giggled and leaned into Quigley's side. His mate draped an arm around him and kissed the top of his head. He looked down the table, happy to see Gram and Hack's grandpa, Moses, talking. Hack's son Elril and David were seated next to each other and seemed to be getting along well. Aster quietly ate her own meal, face serene. Fire could feel her soaking in the threads of connections from the spirit world to help her garner her own impressions of the people seated around her.

He frowned when he noticed Xu watching her like a puppy begging for food. Selene's son was about the same age as Aster, and Fire didn't like that look in his eyes.

"Why are you glaring at Xu?" Sebastian asked quietly from Fire's other side.

"There are threads connecting Aster to Xu," Fire whispered, narrowing his eyes. "Romantic threads."

"They're barely ten," Sebastian said, voice amused.

"He likes her." Fire wrinkled his nose. "She's *my* daughter, and I just got her."

Sebastian smacked Fire's arm. "Don't worry about Xu and Aster. They're just kids. When they get a few years older, you can worry."

"You two aren't as quiet as you think you are," Quigley said, arching a brow.

"Aster's our baby," Fire said, lip trembling.

Quigley gave him a sad look. "She won't always be. I remember singing her to sleep and changing her diapers. Watching her grow into the person she is has been a privilege.

Now, you get to join me in seeing her become an adult. Very slowly. Because she *is* just ten."

Sebastian made a disgusted face. "Why do you have to make me like you?"

Fire rubbed his face on Quigley's shoulder. "Because he's the greatest mate ever."

"I was happy to see you've taken good care of David and Aster," Bowan said, keeping his voice soft as he leaned closer to them. "Several of the more traditional clans still leave any they deem too weak in the deep desert. I've had my own patrols joining Charybdis Station in searching for the abandoned, and somehow I'm still surprised when they find someone."

Quigley's face went hard. "Aster and David aren't weak. They're different, yes, but never weak. Even if they were, there is more to them than their ability to survive in the desert. Aster is my sunrise and always reminds me of the wonder to be found in our world. David's kind nature reminds me that there is more to life than hunting and surviving. They even wanted to abandon Gram, and she is the smartest person I know."

Bowan nodded. "You have a beautiful family, and it makes me happy to know you appreciate them."

Laurie cleared his throat. "I, um, I changed Cyrus's diaper while you were training. Fire explained that you and the little one are both *special*."

Fire tilted his head. "They have birthing lines, Laurie. Remember? They can have babies like you."

Laurie looked panicked for a moment, but Quigley snorted a laugh. "I didn't expect to keep it secret here," Quigley said.

Fire winced. "Oops. Was that a secret? We're going to

Charybdis Station, and people don't care about stuff like that there."

Laurie sighed. "I wish that were the case here. Star's Oasis is much more open-minded than most of the clans, but old beliefs are hard to stomp out." He gave them a nervous look. "I know your clan, Quigley. They are one of the worst. I don't think they'll leave it be."

"We'll be on Charybdis Station," Fire said, sniffing. "The stupid heads can't get us there."

"I think what Laurie is saying is that you should still be careful," Bowan said, wrapping an arm around his mate. "The Burnished aren't tied to our planet anymore. My people keep a close eye on who goes and comes in our spaceport, but we've already had issues with smugglers."

Fire leaned into his mate. "Charybdis Station is safe."

Laurie gave him a strained smile. "I'm sure it is. I think living most of my life with the threat of death constantly hanging over my head makes me more paranoid than others. Just promise me you'll be careful."

"We will," Quigley said, squeezing Fire's hand.

The conversation turned to a lighter topic, but they didn't linger over dinner. Gram and the kids were exhausted, and he wanted some privacy with his mate.

They quickly said their goodbyes and went to the guest wing of the palace.

"We have three rooms," Fire said, bouncing on his toes in front of David's room. "I'll make sure you all have your own space in the attic when we get home, okay?"

Gram chuckled. "We've shared a tent for years. We'll adjust, sweetheart."

"This room's mine," David said, barely opening the door to the middle room. He tried to slide in, but Aster pushed the door all the way open.

"David, why is Gracie in your room?" Quigley asked, giving his son a hard look.

David's eyes widened innocently. "Oh, would you look at that. I'll just let her sleep with me tonight since it's so late, and we don't want to cause a fuss by bringing her outside."

Quigley arched a brow. "Get her lead line. She goes in with the Oryx."

David sighed, shoulders slumping. "I'm sorry, Gracie. I tried."

The goat bleated softly and nudged David's arm. *Love little one.*

Fire danced from foot to foot. "Why can't she stay inside with us? Gracie is family, and she loves David. She's smaller than Perri."

"Perri uses the bathroom outside," Quigley pointed out.

"Just for tonight?" Fire asked, eyes widening as he gave his best puppy dog face.

Quigley groaned. "Okay. Just for tonight. David, you *will* clean that room thoroughly in the morning and take Gracie to stay with our Oryx as soon as you wake up."

David cheered. "Yes, sir."

Aster wrinkled her nose. "I'm glad I'm sharing a room with Gram."

Fire snickered and tugged Quigley next door to their room. "I'll put Cyrus to bed. You get comfortable."

Quigley yawned. "Thanks."

Fire quickly changed Cyrus's diaper and settled him in his bassinet with Cinnamon and Jellybean. "You be a good boy. You can hold Jellybean if you need too, okay? I'll check on you after I get your daddy naked."

He grabbed some lube from his bag, then closed the curtain to the baby's nook. When he turned around, Quigley had finished tugging off his boots and had started to pull off his tunic.

Fire was on him in seconds, wrapping his arms and legs around Quigley and pushing his tongue into his mouth. *Sweet cinnamon sticks, he tastes so good.*

Quigley's hands cupped Fire's ass, and he held him up, their bodies pressed together. "I take it you're ready for this?" he asked between kisses.

"I waited long enough." Fire bit Quigley's lip, then threaded his fingers through Quigley's short hair and pulled his head down for another kiss.

Quigley's hands squeezed Fire's ass, and somehow, they managed to make it to one of the chairs next to the open window. Quigley fell back into the chair, and Fire moved quickly so he was straddling him.

Fire kissed Quigley's neck as he began moving his hips, rubbing his hard dick against his mate. He groaned when Quigley's fingers traced down his spine and slipped into the back of his loose pants.

Fire wasn't sure exactly what he wanted. He'd seen vids and talked to Shae about sex. He knew the basics, but he didn't know what would make the anxious longing in him go away.

"I have my mate in my arms," Quigley said, voice deep and rumbling. "I never thought this would happen, Fire. Thank you for finding me."

Fire's anxiety slowly drained away at Quigley's words and his slow, addictive kisses. *We have plenty of time.*

After a moment, Fire leaned back and pulled off his shirt, then helped Quigley out of his own. Fire kissed the elegantly curved markings covering Quigley's face and neck. They ran over his shoulders, arms and chest, and even dipped into his pants. *Gotta taste them all. It's the law.*

Fire took his time and kissed his way across his Quigley's muscled chest. His hands smoothed across Quigley's broad shoulders, and he nibbled on one of his mate's hardened nipples.

Quigley cupped his head and pulled him up for another wet kiss. "I don't think I was prepared for your mouth on me. I can barely think."

"You can still talk." Fire bit his chin. "I wanna taste you."

He slid down and wedged himself between Quigley's legs. He could see the shape of his mate's dick through his thin, loose pants and leaned forward, pressing his mouth along the thick length.

"Gods," Quigley said and pulled Fire back onto his lap. "Too much of that, and this will be a short evening."

Fire pouted, then slid his pants down, showing off his dark red, lacy underwear.

Quigley's eyes widened as he stared at Fire's erection trapped behind the delicate fabric. "I like your pretty underwear. A lot."

Fire laughed when Quigley gripped his hips and pulled him closer. His mate pressed kisses across his stomach, fingers tracing the lace almost reverently.

A second later, Quigley growled softly and ripped the underwear down the sides, pulling the shreds away.

Fire glared at his mate. "Why did you do that?"

Quigley gave him a sheepish look. "I couldn't help it. I swear they practically told me to do it."

"You talk to underwear?" Fire asked, arching a brow.

Quigley bit his lip and stroked Fire's erection. "Only yours."

Fire shivered at his mate's touch. "Oh, I like that. Okay, I'll forgive you, but no more ripping my pretties."

He straddled Quigley again, pulling Quigley's dick from

his pants and pressing it to his own. He moaned as his fingers circled both of them and stroked up and down, going faster and faster with each movement. *So close, so close, so close.*

Quigley's hand covered his, stopping him, and Fire growled. Then he felt Quigley's lubed finger slipping into his ass. *Oh, that feels different.*

He whimpered as Quigley took his time stretching him. The slight burn of each added finger felt so good. "I'm ready. Promise."

Quigley hummed and slid slowly inside him, hands holding tight to Fire's ass.

Fire gasped at the pain-laced pleasure shooting through him.

Quigley held his hips still and pressed his forehead to Fire's. "Just breath with me, love. You're my flame, my beautiful, fierce flame.

Fire smiled and kissed Quigley. "You're my love muffin."

Quigley groaned. "Do I have to be?"

Fire nodded and buried his face against Quigley's neck, suddenly feeling shy. "My precious love muffin."

Quigley stroked his back and held him as Fire's body adjusted. When Fire was wiggling on his lap, fully enjoying being full of his mate, Quigley started moving, hands gripping Fire's hips as he lifted him, then let Fire slowly slide down his dick.

Fire moaned. "I like this a lot."

Quigley chuckled and arched his hips, hitting something inside Fire that made his blood boil.

"Again," Fire gasped. "Do that again."

Quigley obeyed, twisting his hips and hitting that same spot.

Fire gripped his shoulders and pulled up, sliding back

down Quigley's dick, needing to feel as much as possible. Quigley helped him set a pace, and he rode his mate.

They moved together perfectly, bodies matching each other's movements for seconds or hours – Fire couldn't tell and didn't really care. He bit down on Quigley's bare shoulder when he came, splattering against their stomachs.

Quigley didn't last much longer. His hips bucked up as he came buried in Fire's ass.

They sat for a while, pressed together, cum and sweat quickly drying. Fire didn't want to move. If he moved, then it would end, and he wanted to be that close to his mate forever.

A FEW WEEKS LATER, FIRE HUGGED QUIGLEY AS THEY watched Burnished Outpost grow smaller and smaller as The Blue Solace left the planet behind. The Blue Sparrow and The Black Heron flew beside them, so they occasionally caught glimpses of the other ships.

Fire traced Quigley's jewelry adorned ears and booped the short line of gold hair beads he had talked his mate into wearing. He wanted to give his mate everything in the galaxy.

"Little flame, look at Helara." Quigley watched with wonder as they passed the small moon and quickly picked up speed. "I never could have imagined this. It's one thing to know that there are other worlds above, but to actually see it?"

Fire was more interested in his new family. Aster stood with Kelly. Their arms were linked together, and Kelly whispered to her. Much to Fire's disgust, the two had grown close during their stay at Star's Oasis. Sebastian had already told him that Aster would be joining him and Kelly for shamanism training.

Gram nudged him with her elbow. "Stop glaring at that woman. I really don't know why you don't like her. Now, how long will it take to get to Charybdis Station?"

"Four days," Fire said and yawned. He needed a nap. His mate had worn him out. Fire grinned. He also needed more pretty underwear. Quigley had ruined his last pair the night before. "It just took two days before, but Sebastian said they needed four this time. He looked all weird saying it too."

Jellybean rolled by in his ball, David and Gracie chasing behind him.

Fire smiled at the sound of his son's laughter. He wanted to chase Jellybean too, but there was something he had to do.

"I gotta go talk to Alois," Fire said, leaning up to kiss Quigley's cheek. "I'll be right back."

Quigley nodded, eyes focused on the view outside.

Fire shared an amused look with Gram, then left the room. He rubbed Cyrus's back. The baby was wrapped up close to him again, just the way Fire liked it. Cinnamon curled against Fire's neck, a comforting weight.

He found Alois checking through their inventory. Fire's friend was normally the lieutenant for The Blue Sparrow, but Hack had borrowed him for the trip, mostly so he didn't have to do the boring stuff like inventory himself.

"Alois." Fire put his hands on his hips. "I need a job."

The Dedril turned around slowly and gave him a puzzled look. "You want a job? Why?"

"I have a family to take care of now." Fire sighed heavily. "I gotta expand the attic and put my babies through school. That means I need credits. I can't keep taking yours."

Alois's grin crept across his face. "Fire, you have plenty of credits."

Fire blinked. "I do? When did I get them? Was I sleeping?"

Alois chuckled. "No, you got them the moment you joined us in fighting against the Crellic Queen. Lord Admiral Juren paid you a salary while you were helping us. Sebastian and I have an account set up for you. Plus, Death added credits to it when you all settled down on Charybdis Station. Then, Draif took some and invested it, so now what was in there has almost doubled. You have plenty of money waiting on you."

Fire danced from foot to foot, lip trembling. "I still gotta work. I have to be responsible now. No more naps. I have to wear my serious face now and take care of my family."

Alois set his tablet down and pulled Fire into a hug. "There are a lot of different ways to take care of your family, Fire. Providing the basics for them is only the beginning, and you have that covered. You also need to love and support them, and I think you're going to be really good at that. Talk to Quig, and I bet he'll tell you the same. You'll find the way that works best for you with time, but you don't need to change yourself to do it. You have a lot to offer without wearing your serious face."

Fire swallowed hard. "I can just be me? I'm not like Leti and Sebastian. They're good daddies. What if I forget to feed Cyrus? What if I eat all of David's food? What if I murder Xu because he keeps looking at Aster?"

Alois snorted. "Don't murder Xu, alright? He can't help it that he has his first crush. I overheard him and Rizzie making a plan for Xu to woo Aster. There was something about bows for her kitten and fresh fruit platters. I think they'll be fine."

Fire smacked Alois's chest. "I can't make promises. That's what I'm saying. What if I make a mistake?"

"You will," Alois said, shrugging. "Everyone does. As long as you love those kids, you'll figure it out. Plus, you have Quig. The man is a good dad. He'll help you adjust. You can always come talk to Sebastian and me, or any of our friends on Charybdis Station. You aren't alone."

Fire slowly smiled. "You're right. I've got a big family to help me."

Alois hugged him tight, lifting him off his feet. "You do."

Fire laughed when Cyrus giggled between them and swung his feet. "Put me down. I have to go chase Jellybean."

CHAPTER 8

EN ROUTE TO CHARYBDIS STATION

Quigley panted as he wiped the sweat from his eyes. His body ached from the workout Selene had just put him through. The training sessions with Selene were essential, but they were also a good distraction. So much had happened in the weeks since Sara had died, and he was starting to struggle under the weight of the changes.

His ass protested as he shifted on the hard bench of the training room on the ship. That particular pain wasn't Selene's fault. While he had always been curious, he had never let anyone fuck him before. *My mate asked so nicely,* he thought with a smile, remembering Fire's excitement.

"You're smiling after that?" the man next to him asked. Silas was a large Betonize and good friends with Hack and the others. His husband, Rune, was standing in as the crew medic for The Blue Solace.

"He's newly mated," Hack said with a groan. "Give him a year and his sappy smiles will disappear."

"Really?" Silas asked, arching a brow. "What were you smiling about this morning?"

Hack grinned, eyes filling with heat. "Leti and I finally got a little privacy last night."

Silas shook his head. "Sappy smiles never go away."

A low hiss drew their attention. Leti's Fire Veil dragon watched Quigley closely. The beast had somehow grown larger since it first came in to the training room.

"Princess does *not* like you," Silas said, wincing.

"I'd like to say he was the only one, but there's a large bird in the ship's halls that dives at me every time I have to leave a room." Quigley sighed. "A lot of the pets are protective of Fire. He says to give them time, and they'll warm up to me."

Princess hissed again.

Hack shrugged. "Princess eventually warmed up to me after I mated Leti. Now we get along well."

The dragon turned his stare at Hack, and small puffs of smoke drifted from his nostrils.

"Don't you look at me like that," Hack said, raising a brow. "I have to give up part of my bed for you every night."

"Break's over," Selene interrupted, voice emotionless. "Back to work."

Hack whimpered. "Selene, why do you hate us?"

She tilted her head and considered Hack. "You spend too much time in the Council chambers now that you're a general. You're getting out of shape."

Her cat, a very fluffy calico named Fluffle, stared at Hack, eyes judging.

Hack sniffed. "Rude."

Quigley slowly stood. "I've gotten complacent too. I *know* hunting and fighting with other Burnished. There is so much I don't know."

Selene nodded at him. "You learn quickly and aren't afraid to work hard."

Fluffle gave him an approving look, then stalked back to the training mats to wait for them.

Silas stood and started stretching. "Do you think you'll join the Blue Fleet, Quig?"

Quigley thought for a moment. "I don't know. I enjoy hunting."

Hack gave him a considering look. "What about enforcement? They patrol the station, but they also investigate disturbances and help keep the peace. Mom was complaining the other day that she needed more recruits."

Silas grinned. "We really do. If you're interested in enforcement, I can start going over some of the routine procedures with you. It's not hunting as you know it, but believe me when I tell you our prey is far more challenging than a jackrabbit."

Quigley flushed. "I would appreciate that."

Offering another Burnished help was *not* something the people in his previous clan did. Hunters searched for food for their own family. While they offered a portion to the clan elder, they did not share freely.

His mate's friends and family were very different, and Quigley couldn't help but feel honored to be where he was.

The doors opened, and Jellybean rolled inside, pushing his ball forward. He stopped and squeaked at Quigley a moment before rolling out a different door.

Hack sighed. "That's life on The Blue Solace."

Quigley heard Fire and David's laughter before he saw them. His mate had Cyrus strapped to his chest and Cinnamon on his shoulder. David and Gracie ran with him.

Fire ran to him and kissed his cheek. "Where's Jellybean? We got distracted by snacks and lost him."

"He went out the other door," Quigley answered.

"It goes to the bridge," Hack said with a yawn.

"Thanks. Fluffle, train them well," Fire said.

Fluffle meowed softly and nodded at Fire.

"Gotta go." Fire grinned and waved goodbye before following Jellybean.

Quigley grabbed David before he followed and hugged him tight. "Don't forget to clean up after Gracie, son."

David nodded. "I do. Sometimes these little bots clean up her poop before I can, but usually it's me."

"Good boy." Quigley kissed the top of his head and set him on his feet. "Have fun."

David grinned wide and ran for the door with Gracie.

Hack eyed him. "You don't mind that Fire spends his days playing with the pets and babies?"

Quigley shook his head. "It's who he is, and I would never want to change that. Helara has blessed me."

Hack smacked his shoulder. "Good to hear. Fire isn't like anyone else on the station, but he's an important part of our family. I'm glad you recognize that."

"Enough talk." Selene tossed Quigley and Hack vibro-swords. "It's time for close-quarters combat."

LATER THAT NIGHT, QUIGLEY SLIPPED INTO HIS ROOM, utterly exhausted from the long day. Somehow, Fire and he had ended up with a private room. The kids were sharing a large room with all the other children on the ship, and Gram was keeping an eye on them with other volunteers.

Fire was already there. He sat at the table next to a small window, a large platter of food in front of him. "I brought us dinner. Our babies are having a cupcake party with the other kids."

Quigley smiled. "Thank you, little flame."

Fire smiled widely, pure happiness pouring from him. "Aster snuck me a couple cupcakes. I ate one, but I saved the other for you."

Quigley smiled, his tiredness and worry lightening. That happened often when his mate was around. "Thanks."

Fire stood and guided him to sit down before crawling into Quigley's lap. "Jellybean and Cinnamon are already sleeping. Cinnamon got in trouble today because he kept sitting on Princess Buttercup's head, and Princess got annoyed and tried to set him on fire. Cinnamon moved before he got hurt, but Leti yelled at Princess, which hurt Princess's feelings. He just didn't want Cinnamon on his head. I made Cinnamon apologize, but I don't think he was all that sincere. I have a feeling he'll be sitting on Princess's head a lot."

Quigley fed Fire a bite of the seasoned chicken and laughed. "They sound like brothers. One always has to do his best to annoy the other. Sara was a terror when she was a kid. She—" He stopped suddenly, grief hitting him hard.

Fire cupped his face. "Quig?"

"She's dead." Quigley gasped, pain shooting through him. "She won't get to meet you or see Cyrus grow up. She didn't get to see Helara from space or the inside of a spaceship. She won't get a new life on Charybdis Station."

Fire's lip trembled, and his eyes filled with tears. "I wish I had found you sooner. I could have saved her."

"We shouldn't have needed saving." Quigley felt like his soul was full of rocks weighing him down. "Tragedies happen. People die, and we lose the ones we love. That's life."

"I don't like it," Fire said, voice dark. "It's stupid."

"It is," Quigley whispered. He pulled Fire closer and hugged him as tightly as he could. His mate squeaked but hugged him back. "Gram says things happen for a reason, and that the gods know better than us. That helps her deal with losing family, but I can't believe that. Sara deserved to see all of this. She deserved a lifemate of her own."

"Tell me about her?" Fire asked, voice barely above a whisper.

Quigley swallowed hard. "I've tried not to think about her since they killed her. We had to push forward. To survive."

"You get to rest now," Fire said, stroking his fingers through Quigley's hair. "The bad memories come when we least expect them."

Quigley nodded, closing his eyes. He buried his face against Fire's neck and savored his mate's spicy cinnamon scent. "She was a wild child. Sara loved going on hunts and exploring the desert."

"Like you," Fire said, kissing Quigley's cheek.

"She was better with people than me. I hated talking to the other Burnished, so I stuck to myself. Sara, though, could make anyone like her. She had friends and was a true part of the clan." Quigley huffed out a laugh and opened his eyes. "Despite that, her loyalty was with her family. She knew about my birthing line and never told anyone. She never made me feel like less of a person because of it."

"Rune checked you over and said you can have babies," Fire said, shaking his head. "You can create another person in your body. Why would that be bad?"

"Families turn on one another all the time," Quigley said, voice sad. "In our clan, traditions run deep. If someone had discovered my birthing line, they wouldn't just kill me. They would have killed all who had hid it."

Fire scowled. "I should have let Fire Fluffle eat them."

Quigley gave him a tired smile. "I wouldn't have minded that, but I'm glad you didn't. I don't want you to have to kill anyone ever again. I'm not the only one with bad memories."

Fire bit his lip, thinking of the nightmare he had two nights ago. He had been on a long forgotten battlefield, following his queen's orders to scorch the approaching Crellic army. "You don't mind that I'm not a warrior?"

"I want you to be exactly the person you are," Quigley said, kissing his mate's neck. "My happy little flame."

Fire scooped up a bite of the rice dish on the platter and fed it to him. "I've seen a lot of families during my cycles. Some actually enjoyed hurting each other. Then, even the *good* ones sometimes were stupid. Parents tried to force their children to act a certain way and got mad when their children weren't perfect. Then those kids would treat their own babies the same way. It was always about being whatever their society wanted them to be. Look this way. Act this way." Fire scowled. "All they had to do was love their babies. Sometimes that wasn't enough, but a lot of times it was."

Quigley thought about Aster and David. "It really isn't complicated, is it? My clan wanted to leave Aster and David in the deep desert when they were born, but I just wanted to love them. Now, I can't imagine life without them. Gods, I can't imagine a life without Gram in it. Sara and I grew up well, but without Gram, we would have been miserable."

Fire nodded. "Love is what's important, and Gram loves you all. Now I'm here too, and you aren't alone anymore. I'll take care of you and our babies. I'll bring you yummy food and make sure you always smile. If anyone upsets you... Well you've met Fluffle, and he's my friend."

Quigley chuckled. "See? All I need is you."

CHAPTER 9

CHARYBDIS STATION, ANCHORS REST
SYSTEM

Fire held Jellybean and Cyrus in his arms and watched Quigley's face as they approached Charybdis Station. Quigley, the kids, and Gram all watched the station in fascination.

Fire remembered when he first saw it. The planet-sized station was a beautiful work of metal and pure life. He didn't know how the engineers had done it, but he did know that the station spoke to him like Genarg had. It had a curious nature that Fire could appreciate.

"It's beautiful," Quigley said softly. His mate looked different dressed in one of Hack's uniforms. His pants clung to the muscles in his thighs and ass, and the tight black vest bared his beautiful markings for all the galaxy to see.

Cinnamon perched on top of Quigley's head, almost disappearing in the black curls that Fire's mate had let grow since they met. Quigley shivered, and Fire spun around, searching for the coat he'd bought his mate. He found it on the lounge beside Kelly.

"Need a coat," he said, shoving her a little so he could reach it.

"I could have handed it to you," she said, rolling her eyes.

"Then I wouldn't have gotten to shove you," Fire said, sticking his tongue out at her. *Can't let her know I like her now*, he thought.

Fire helped Quigley slip the coat on.

"It feels strange to be cold all the time," Quigley said, flushing. "You and the others don't need a coat."

Gram pulled her own warm shawl around her. "They didn't spend their whole lives on a hot desert planet. They say we'll adjust in time."

Fire leaned over and kissed her cheek. "I'll keep the attic nice and toasty for you, Gram."

She chuckled and patted his arm. "That's alright, Fire. Moses over there offered to help me stay warm."

Quigley glared at Hack's grandpa. "What?"

Gram smacked Quigley's side. "Don't start that shit, young man. I've been alone a long time, and Moses is nice company."

Fire's eyes widened. "Oh. You and Grandpa Moses are gonna have sex. That warms Quig up too, Gram. His skin gets all glisteny and tastes yummy. Good idea."

Quigley squeezed his eyes shut when the people around them started laughing. "They maybe didn't need to know that about me, little flame."

Fire shrugged and hugged Quigley. "I feel sorry for them 'cause they don't get to see you naked like I do."

Aster groaned. "Kelly, save me."

Kelly chuckled. "Come on. We'll be landing soon, so let's go get the Oryx ready."

"Gracie shouldn't have to hear this either," David said, wrinkling his nose and tugging his goat's lead line. "I like being naked, same as the next guy, but glisteny and yummy aren't words I want to hear describe Dad."

Fire rocked Cyrus and Jellybean. "They don't know what they're missing."

Quigley sighed and wrapped Fire in his arms, watching the station get closer. "Tell me who we'll meet today."

Fire ran a finger down one of Cyrus's long ears. He didn't understand how something so big could still be so tiny. *Babies are special.*

"Fire?" Quigley sounded amused.

"Oh, okay, so you'll meet Ma and Pops Brakenstone. They're my friend Beck's parents, and they love me a lot. Ma makes really good casseroles, and Pops gives the best dad hugs. Beck and his mate will be there too. Beck is really sweet and so is Beol. I like to visit Dr. Bloop and he lives with them. So do all their babies. Aketil is their oldest and she's Crellic. She likes to explore the station with me, but Beck or Beol get mad when I take her with me without telling them."

"That's a lot of people," Quigley said, voice nervous.

Fire kissed his cheek. "That's just some of them. Fasi and Renee will be there too because they love me and want to meet you and the kids."

"Your clan leaders." Quigley took a deep breath and let it out slowly. "I'll show them respect."

"Then there's Death," Fire said, fighting back a yawn. "He said he needed to look you over. He's my favorite brother friend and loves me too. He looks kinda scary, but don't worry. He's really nice. His mate, Val, always makes sure they have my favorite mustard for when I come make sandwiches at their house. Scythe lives there too, and he's super snuggly and almost as good at naps as Marmalade."

Sebastian snorted from where he stood behind them. "I can't wait for you to meet Death. He can see souls, you know. He'll be able to tell exactly what kind of person you really are, and he can also harvest your soul in an instant." He snapped his fingers. "One second you're alive and aware. The next you're an empty, soulless husk."

Quigley stiffened in his arms, and Fire leaned up to kiss him again. "It's true. Death can summon spirits and control them too, but he doesn't like to do that. He says it's mean. Instead he just avoids them."

"That's nice," Quigley said, voice sounding strained.

Sebastian's laugh didn't sound very nice, so Fire turned around and glared at him. "You told me yesterday that you like Quigley. Remember?"

Sebastian winced. "You're not supposed to tell him that. I'm just having a little fun with him. You only meet your mate's family one time."

"It's not nice fun." Fire narrowed his eyes. "I'm going to make Woolly sleep with you tonight."

Sebastian groaned. "That kitten is so mean to anyone except Aster. How can something so cute be so evil?"

Alois watched Fluffle stalk past them. "I ask myself that after every encounter with Fluffle."

Fire gasped. "Fluffle isn't evil. Fluff is the greatest protector in the galaxy. Take it back, Alois."

Fluffle gave Alois a smug look, and the man rolled his eyes. "Okay, okay. Fluffle isn't completely evil. He just scares me."

Quigley jerked beside him when the ship started its descent into the spaceport. "I'll never get used to ships."

"You all have done a lot better than I expected," Alois said. "Bigger ships are better than shuttles."

As soon as the clamps latched onto the ship, Fire put Jellybean on Quigley's shoulder, then tugged him to the ramp. "I bet Ma cooked a big dinner for us. She probably made cake too."

Quigley looked around. "Do we have to go first?"

Fire bounced in place until the ramp lowered. "Look, it's Dr. Bloop! Hi, Dr. Bloop. This is my mate, Quigley, and look at my baby. This is Cyrus. Aren't his ears precious?"

Beck and Beol's dog grinned at him, tongue hanging out. *Family? Family is good.*

"They're the best family ever." Fire nodded. "You'll like them when you get to know them. Hi, Luna. This is my mate, Quigley."

Wyatt and Morgan's dog sniffed Quigley's ankle, then settled her paw on his foot. *Mate smells good. I like him.*

"Thank you, Luna," Fire said, pride filling him. "He's a little shy, so make sure you snuggle him if you have time. Quig needs lots of love. Okay?"

Luna leaned against Quigley's leg and let him pet her. *I'll snuggle him.*

Honey and Stardust flew clumsily to him and landed in front of Quigley. *Mate?* Honey sent him the image of Draif and Lucas entwined together on the couch.

"Exactly," Fire said and introduced the two baby dragons to Quigley.

Someone cleared their throat, and Fire turned around. "Oh, it's Fasi. Quigley, come meet Fasi. He gives good hugs too."

Fasi chuckled and pulled him into a gentle hug. "I'll try not to squish the baby."

Fire turned Cyrus to face his friend. "Look at those chubby cheeks. Cy loves kisses."

Fasi bent and kissed the baby's cheek. The large purple Grell looked fierce, but he was soft and mushy inside. "He's beautiful, Fire. I'm so happy for you and know you'll make a wonderful dad. Now, introduce me to your mate."

Quigley gave Fasi a solemn look and nodded. "I'm Quigley.

I'm a good hunter and have been training with Selene and Silas to join the station's enforcement. I will work hard to contribute to Charybdis Station if you allow me and my family to stay."

Fasi blinked a few times, then guided Fire and Cyrus to Renee. "'If I'll allow you to stay'?" He hugged Quigley tightly, lifting the large Burnished off his feet. "Son, you're already family."

Fire hugged Renee and giggled. "Quig's face is all red."

The small Havenite woman snorted. "That just means he needs more hugs in his life, doesn't it?"

Fire nodded. "You'll watch out for him when he joins enforcement?"

Renee patted his cheek. "Of course I will. Silas has already made it clear he wants your mate as his partner after he finishes training."

"Fire." Shae ran through the crowded spaceport. Fire's friend was a slender Siren with elegant horns. "I wanted to be here right when you landed. Damn, is that your mate hugging Fasi? He is gorgeous."

Fire grinned smugly. "I did good, huh?"

"You certainly did," Shae said and hugged him. "How is everything going?"

"You were right about sex." Fire squeezed Shae tightly. "It's a lot of fun."

Renee snorted. "I really don't want to know what the two of you talk about."

"Shae's the only one that will tell me things." Fire kissed Shae's cheek. "Sex really was fun, but snuggling is the best. I think if my dick hadn't liked Quig like that, I would still be happy as his mate."

"I love that heart of yours," Shae said, giving him a fond look. "I'm glad you found him."

"Me too." He heard a familiar bleat and turned around. Gracie stood with David and Aster. The kids looked a little overwhelmed at the sheer number of people coming and going around the spaceport.

Kelly stood behind them, one hand settled on Aster's shoulder and the reins of the Oryx in her other.

"Renee, Shae, these are my other babies. This is Aster, our sunrise, and David, our sweet boy." Fire pulled Renee to them. "That's Gracie, David's goat."

David scowled. "I'm not sweet."

Fire bent and hugged him. "You can't hide it, David. Just embrace the sweetness. Make it your own."

David sighed. "I guess I can be like you. I want to talk to the animals too."

"Oh, goodness, look at all these beautiful children of yours." Ma Brakenstone pushed past Renee and grabbed Aster in a hug. "You're just so precious, sweetheart."

Aster gasped, face full of shock. She hugged Ma back. "You feel so beautiful."

Ma tilted her head and gave Aster a fond look. "What, dearie?"

"Aster feels things from the spirit world," Fire explains. "She can feel you, and you really do feel beautiful, Ma. Like cinnamon apple strudel."

"Hey, I want a hug," David said, pulling on Aster's leg. "You have to share Ma, Aster."

Ma chuckled and pulled David into her arms too. "Oh, you are a sweetie."

"Dang it," David muttered. He settled his head on her shoulder and closed his eyes. "Just embrace it, David."

Shae snickered. "Stars, he is definitely your son."

Pops Brakenstone moved to stand beside him. He hugged

Fire and Cyrus. "Fasi hasn't let your mate go yet, and I'm not sure he's gonna."

Fire looked around. Fasi still had Quigley in a hug and was whispering to him. Jellybean still balanced on his shoulder, but he chittered excitedly at Quigley too.

"I knew Fasi would like him." Fire smiled proudly. "My mate is the best. Oh, Pops, we're gonna have to expand the attic. Can you help? I have my three babies and Gram to make room for. Wait. Where's Gram?"

"I believe that's her speaking with Death," Renee said, voice dry. "It looks like she's lecturing him."

Fire shrugged. "Okay. So, I need some more space, Pops."

Pops grinned. "Don't you worry one bit about that. We have a surprise for you."

Fire gasped. "I love surprises."

Fasi finally put Quigley down when Death approached them. Fire's fellow Element looked like he had swallowed a lemon.

"I've been ordered to be nice to you, Burnished," Death said, glaring at Quigley. "Gram was quite insistent."

"My grandson is a good boy," Gram said, hands on her hips. "No taking his soul."

"As you wish," Death said with a sigh. "It's such a lovely soul too. Brave, honest, and loving. The kindness shining from him practically blinds me anyway."

"Veri," Death's mate, Val, said with a laugh. "Stop teasing them. Gram, he doesn't take people's souls unless they're attacking him or something like that."

Fire smiled proudly. "His soul is pretty, right, Death? My mate has the prettiest soul ever, doesn't he?"

"I'm sure you've seen a glimpse of it in the spirit world,"

Death said, giving him a half smile. "Please don't make me say he has a pretty soul."

Sebastian hurried to them, Mordy balanced on his hip. "Have you threatened him yet? Did I miss it?"

Death's smile was a little feral. "I was just about—"

Gram cleared her throat. "You were just about to give my grandson a big hug and welcome him to the family, weren't you?"

Death's smile faded into a scowl. "I don't hug."

Val sighed and hugged Quigley. "I apologize for my mate. He's a bit overprotective of Fire, but he knows you're a good person. He can tell that right away. He just has to come to terms with the fact that his little brother is now mated."

"Hey, Val." Fire held up Cyrus. "Look at my baby. He's just a few months younger than Seshi. Do you think they'll be best friends?" Fire looked down. Seshi was sleeping in his stroller, a ghost guinea pig curled up at his side. "Hi, Marshmallow. See my baby?"

Marshmallow squeaked softly. *Family beautiful.*

"Thank you." Fire sighed happily. "I'm gonna be a good daddy."

Ma carried David and Aster to them. "I'm sure you will, Fire. Let's get moving. Pops and I want to show you the surprise."

Sebastian whined low in his throat. "That's it? No death threats or bodily harm? Quigley's taking my son from me. He took Fire's flower of innocence. Shouldn't we at least rough him up a bit?"

Fire gasped, ignoring his friends' laughter around him. "Quig, did you take my flower? I didn't even know I had a flower. Give it back." *I'll name it, Delores,* he thought excitedly.

Quigley flushed. "I don't think he means an actual flower, but you all are so strange, so maybe he does."

"What kind of flower is it?" Fire asked Sebastian. "Is it part of our surprise? Ma, is food our surprise?"

Sebastian groaned. "Stars this is more painful for me than stupid Quigley. Let's just get on the tram."

CHAPTER 10

Quigley held Fire's hand as they followed the large group from the spaceport. There were so many people around them, and he counted at least twenty ships that were in view. He saw very few Burnished, but there were several other species, some he recognized and some he didn't.

Fire continued to introduce him to people and pets, but Quigley had long passed the point of being able to follow along.

His attention was split between the conversation and observing everything around him. There were metals and other material, which he expected, but there was so much green as well. Trees, shrubs, and flowers were everywhere. They even passed an endless looking field of crops.

The sheer wealth of resources around Quigley shocked him. The way everyone had described space stations had made him think they would be like living in a different type of desert.

The thrum of energy beneath his feet was unlike anything he had felt before. He missed the comforting familiar of

Burnished Outpost, but he thought he might get used to this new planet of metal and magic.

After the quick ride on the tram, Fasi and Pops led them into a large encampment. *Neighborhood,* he reminded himself. *Fire calls it the neighborhood.*

Houses of all different colors lined the street, each with flowers and trees surrounding them. The large path the led through it was lined with even more flowers.

"Here's our first stop," Ma said gesturing to a large fenced-in area. Three animals watched them from inside. One he recognized as a goat like Gracie, but the other two he had never seen before.

"Hi, Wobble," Fire said, waving.

Leti pushed forward and hugged the long-necked creature. "Did you miss me? You're going to have a new sister named Salsa. She's on her way here now, and I just know you'll love her."

"That's his llama," Fire whispered. "The other two are Muffin and Trixie."

"We expanded the pasture, so you can keep Gracie and your Oryx close by." Fasi grinned and patted Quigley's back. "Leti needed more space anyway, and his critters get along with just about everyone."

Fire squealed and hugged Fasi. "Thank you. Quig loves his Oryx, and I was worried we would have to keep him in Death and Val's backyard."

"Why my backyard?" Death asked, scowling.

"Because Sebby's already belongs to Wobble, Trixie, and Muffin," Fire answered, rolling his eyes and making Quigley laugh.

"Thank you, sir," Quigley said with a nod to Fasi. "Please let me know how to repay you."

Fasi gave him a hard look. "You need another hug, don't you?"

Before Quigley knew it, he was back in the large Grell's arms. It wasn't a bad place to be. Fasi had a way of making Quigley feel like everything was going to be alright. The problem was, it was hard to deal with the comfort.

With Fire's hugs, Quigley could focus on having his mate in his arms. With the kids, it was about *him* offering them comfort. With Gram, it was about facing the new changes together.

A hug from this man, this leader, made Quigley want to let go of the stress and worry. It made him want to let himself mourn Sara. *I really don't want to break down in front of everyone*, he thought, trying to force away his tears.

Sebastian wiggled between Fasi and Quigley and pushed them apart. He kept his hand on Quigley's chest but watched Fasi. "Let's finish with the surprises and get to the food. I'm hungry."

Fasi huffed, then gave Sebastian a kiss. "So bossy."

Ma and Pops took the lead and the others followed. Fire stole Jellybean from Quigley's shoulder and ran ahead with David and Aster.

Sebastian gave him a sad look once they were alone. "I can't believe I missed it. Who are you mourning?"

Quigley shook his head. "There's no time for this. The others are waiting."

Sebastian's hand clenched in his shirt. "Give me a name and I'll let you follow them."

Quigley closed his eyes, his sister's mischievous smile filling his mind. "Sara. My sister. She would have liked it here."

Sebastian sighed. "Fasi's hugs are a little too comforting, huh? They've always been like that for me too. It's hard to stay strong when that man's telling you he loves you and will take care of everything bothering you."

"Yes," Quigley managed to say.

"We better catch up before they get to your surprise," Sebastian said, linking his arm with Quigley's.

Quigley's eyes flew open, and he looked at the other man in surprise. "What's happening here?"

Sebastian gave him a disgusted look. "I'm admitting I like you, okay? I'll tell Mustachio to stop dive bombing you."

"I knew he was doing that because of you." Quigley fought a laugh. He felt Cinnamon adjust his weight on Quigley's head. He had gotten so used to the black stinger sitting there that he had almost forgotten the little guy.

"Well, that little monster on top of your head has your back." Sebastian gave him a reluctant smile. "I keep waking up to find him watching me like he's about to sting me."

Quigley smiled and gentle patted Cinnamon's back. "Good boy."

They caught up with the rest of the group. Everyone had stopped to gawk at a lovely sandstone home that looked almost exactly like one of the nicer houses in Star's Oasis. It stood out from the rest around it, but Quigley thought it was the nicest in the neighborhood.

"This wasn't here when we left," Fire said, eyes wide. He pointed to the dark blue house next door. "That's Sebby's house." He pointed to the yellow one on the other side. "That's Juniper's house."

"This is your house," Pops said, smiling proudly. "Val and I designed it as soon as we heard you had a mate. Then everyone pitched in to get it built. The landscaping could use some work, but Kelly wanted to do something special with it."

The woman grinned. "You're going to love the flowers I'm going to grow you, Fire."

Fire gave her a suspicious look. "Can I name *them* Delores?"

"Sure." Kelly patted Aster's shoulder. "I have a bunch of aster flowers that I'm going to plant too. I'm also going to make the perfect blend of grasses for Gracie and the Oryx in the back yard."

Quigley stared at the large house in front of him. *They did all of this for Fire?* He had known they were fond of his mate, but this was surprising.

Sebastian leaned closer. "I know how you feel. Fasi had this whole neighborhood built for Leti before he had even met him in person. These people take love to the extreme, and it's better if you just go with it instead of fighting them."

"We won't be living in your home," he said softly. "Fire will miss that."

Sebastian watched Fire fondly. "I'll miss it too, but sometimes kids grow up and start their own families."

Fire's eyes found Quigley's and he waved. "We have a house. Gram won't have to share with Gracie."

Gram snorted. "Good thing or we'd be having roast goat for dinner."

"Gram," David said, covering Gracie's ears. "Language."

Ma chuckled and rubbed a hand over David's head. "This seems a good time to tell you I made a welcome home dinner. It's inside."

Fire whooped and ran for the door. "Cyrus and me are starving."

"Me too. Me too." David quickly followed, leading Gracie behind him.

"When is that not the case?" Kelly asked, linking her arm with Aster. "Brothers are so obnoxious."

"They are," Aster agreed, sighing.

Quigley smiled for a moment, remembering Sara saying that exact thing. Then he realized David had just brought his goat into their new home. "Damn it, David. Gracie lives outside."

LATER THAT NIGHT, QUIGLEY SAT ALONE WITH FIRE ON THE couch in their living room. Gram was already settled comfortably in her own room on the first floor of the house while Aster and David both had rooms upstairs. Pops and Ma had even made Cyrus a nursery, which confused Quigley a bit. Babies didn't need an entire room, but they all seemed to think Cy did.

"I only got one nap today," Fire said, yawning. "Jellybean says you need at least three naps a day to be happy."

"Jellybean also spent the day rubbing his butt all over the house." Quigley shook his head. "I love him, but he's a strange piggy."

"He was marking his territory." Fire leaned against his arm. "Will you do the thing?"

Quigley smiled and held his hand up. He called a small flame to dance on his palm.

Fire sighed and ran his hand through the flame, causing it to grow and twist in a beautiful dance. "I love the feel of your fire."

"It's all yours." Quigley sunk deeper in the soft couch and let himself relax as Fire played with the dancing flame.

His mate was so different than anyone he had ever met. Fire seemed to find the good in everything and everyone around him.

"Cinnamon likes the Druffle," Fire said, nodding to where a nest of small balls of fluff lived.

Cinnamon watched them travel through the tube-shaped tunnels covering one wall of the living room. The black stinger was likely imagining eating them, but Quigley didn't think Fire would appreciate knowing that.

"Renee said you could start training with enforcement tomorrow." Fire sighed heavily. "Can't you just stay with me instead? I'll show you all the best places to get food. Juniper's house is the very best because they always have tasty leftovers, but Cordelia is actually a good cook too, and Leti and Sebastian don't know it, so there's usually more leftovers at her house. Finn's house is the best place for finding pretty underwear. He buys me pairs all the time and even made me my own undie basket. I think he just didn't want me digging through his clothes."

Quigley smiled against Fire's hair. He would have thought Fire's friends were tired of the man breaking into their houses and taking their food and clothes, but they had made it very clear to Quigley that Fire could do whatever Fire wanted.

Which reminds me. "You told me Beol was nice," Quigley said. "You didn't tell me he led a clan of assassins."

"He's a nice assassin," Fire said, yawning, his sleepy eyes watching the dancing flame. "Are you going to like being in enforcement?"

"I think so," Quigley said. "I need to be able to serve the station, and I like the idea of it. I'll know more when I finish training."

"Are you sure I don't need to find a job?" Fire asked, voice small. "Do I need to serve the station too?"

"You do serve the station," Quigley said, hugging his mate. "Remember the story I told you about Helara?"

Fire nodded, eyes focused on the flame.

"Helara wasn't a warrior or a leader. He was the heart of the clan. You're the heart of our family, of this neighborhood really." Quigley closed his fist and the flame disappeared. He tilted Fire's chin so his mate met his gaze. "You're my heart, Fire. You don't have to do anything but be yourself."

"I love you too," Fire whispered, smiling wide.

Quigley leaned in for a kiss. Life would be different, but with Fire by his side, it could only be better.

TWO MONTHS LATER

Fire held Cyrus up. "Cy needs kisses."

Quigley smiled and kissed the baby's cheeks.

Fire moved Cyrus to his hip and held up Jellybean. "Jellybean needs kisses."

Quigley snorted a laugh and kissed the guinea pig on the head. "Of course he does."

Jellybean squeaked. *I didn't need a kiss.*

Fire set Jellybean down and reached for Cinnamon. "One more."

Quigley arched a brow. "I'm *not* kissing a black stinger. Cinnamon doesn't want one anyway. He's a stoic little guy."

Cinnamon stared at Quigley. *I do need a kiss.*

Quigley narrowed his eyes. "How is it possible for him to look cute?"

"Kiss, kiss, kiss." Fire waved Cinnamon in the air.

Quigley sighed and dipped to kiss the black stinger. "There. All done."

Fire settled Cinnamon on Quigley's head. "Have a good first day at work."

"Dad," David yelled from the door. "Silas is here."

Quigley gave Fire a brief kiss. "I love you, little flame. Have a good day."

Fire kept his lips firmly pressed together. He had a secret and didn't want to blurt it out. "I will."

Quigley gave him a suspicious look, then left, pausing to hug David at the door.

"You didn't tell him," Aster said. Fire's daughter curled up on a chair in the living room, her tablet in her lap. She had quickly discovered a love of books and music now that she had the time and technology to indulge in them.

Woolly slept on the back of the chair, looking sweet and innocent in sleep. *Little monster*, Fire thought fondly. The kitten adored Aster but barely tolerated everyone else.

"He has to know I'm going to tell everyone today," Fire said, bouncing in place. "We're gonna have another baby."

More babies, Jellybean squeaked before starting his morning dance. He ran a short distance, then jumped in the air. He landed on all fours and bounced up again before turning the other way to repeat his morning ritual.

"What did you just say?" David asked, eyes wide. "Dad's pregnant? Come on, Gracie. We gotta go tell Elril."

Fire winced as David's goat looked up from where she worked on chewing the couch. "Remember you have to get to — And they're out the door."

"Elril will make sure he gets to class on time. I'm glad David and he are best friends because he's a lot more responsible than David." Aster smiled. "Enough of that though. What are you hiding? You feel like secrets this morning."

"Quig misses the sunrise over the desert." Fire's shoulders slumped, and he moved closer so he could run a hand through her long braids. It always soothed him. "You're his sunrise, but not actually a sunrise."

Aster giggled. "I'm glad you figured that out. He likes watching the sun rise over the station too."

"It's just a little glow at the edge of the big atmosphere thingies," Fire said, pouting. "It's not the same."

"He'd rather have you than sunrises," Aster said, smiling softly.

"Maybe, but I'm going to get him a desert sunrise today," Fire said, putting his serious face on. "After I go get Juniper's leftover broccoli and cheese casserole. I gotta hurry because Leti has plans to steal it."

Aster hummed low. "Can you get some of that sweet potato stuff too? I really like it."

Fire hugged her. "I'll always provide for my family. Have you thought more about what we talked about?"

Aster's face grew pensive. "I don't know. Right now, I'm just trying to get used to all of the changes. I don't think I could handle suddenly being able to see too. Dad says I'm fine just how I am, so it's up to me if I want to change it."

Wyatt had examined Aster, then consulted with a specialist. They could do a transplant that would allow Aster to see. Quigley and Fire just wanted Aster to be happy, whether that was with or without sight was up to her.

"He's so smart." Fire hummed appreciatively. "My smart, yummy mate."

She laughed and stood. "I'm going to go see Kelly before school."

"Thank you, Aster. Tell Kelly I hate her."

"I always do," Aster said, smirking. "She'll just say she hates you too."

An hour later, Fire waved goodbye as Aster and David piled onto the school tram with the rest of the neighborhood kids.

David held Pepper's hand as she did her best to hide a

much smaller Aagy in her sweater. She had only been attending school a few days now, but she had managed to sneak Aagy with her each day. David had complained that Gracie wouldn't fit in his pocket.

Fire scowled when he noticed that Xu kept a close eye on Aster as she moved to sit down next to Rizzie. It made Fire want to set the boy's shoes on fire.

"Be nice," Parker, Selene's mate, said and nudged Fire in the side. "Xu can't help it that he's in love with Aster."

Fire pouted. "Whatever."

Leti laughed. "Rizzie says he keeps leaving Aster gifts, but won't even try talking to her. It's starting to frustrate Rizzie. She doesn't get why they can't just talk it out."

"Because they're babies and there's nothing to talk out," Fire said, pouting. "I gotta go provide for my family."

Leti's eyes widened. "Wait, I want that broccoli and cheese casserole, damn it."

Fire switched Cyrus to his other hip and bolted for Juniper's house. "Too late."

"Milo, attack," Leti said, pointing his finger at Fire.

Leti's youngest looked at Fire and grinned before waving. "Bye-bye."

"Sugar cookies," Leti yelled. "I should have brought Princess with me."

Fire made it to Juniper's in record time and typed in his friend's security code. "Time for some yum-yums, Cy." He had the casserole and sweet potatoes stacked in his free arm by the time Leti reached the door with Milo in tow. "Sorry, you're too slow. There's some turkey left, but that's it."

Leti groaned. "You have to pick up the pace, Milo."

Milo plopped down on the floor and started to glow with his inner flames.

"Poop it," Leti said, kneeling down. "No fire, baby boy. We don't want to set Juniper's house on fire."

Milo giggled but stopped glowing.

"Why did I want so many kids?" Leti asked, sighing.

"Because you're the Blue Angel of Charybdis Station." Fire kissed Leti's cheek. "Oh, by the way, Quig is pregnant. I'm gonna have another baby."

Leti's face filled with joy, and he squealed. "Have you told Sebastian? We need to tell Sebastian. What about Shae?"

Fire sighed. "Let me bring my catch home and store it for later. Sebby probably has some pecan pie left over from last night. I think it'll go well with dinner."

Leti snorted and picked Milo back up. "I'm telling him now. Come on, Milo. Time to run."

Fire took his time walking back to his house and putting the food in the refrigerator. Gram was awake and nursing a cup of coffee at the table. With the treatments Charybdis Station offered, her bones didn't hurt too much, and she enjoyed sleeping in every morning. She also spent way too much time with Grandpa Moses. Well, *Quigley* thought she spent way too much time with him.

"How many people have you told so far?" she asked, amused.

"Just two," he said defensively. "Leti is telling Sebastian now."

His back door slammed open, and Sebastian rushed in. "Quigley's pregnant? I'm going to be a grandpa? Oh gods, I'm too young to be a grandpa."

Gram chuckled. "Death did all kinds of tests with that fancy tech of his and found out the baby will have Fire's eyes and likely a dose of his power. She'll also have Quigley's ears." Gram shook her head. "He can already tell all that and the baby is just a little dot in Quig's body."

"She?" Sebastian's eyes grew wide, and his bottom lip trembled.

"We're gonna name her Sara Sebina," Fire said, feeling sad for a moment. "Quig misses his sister a lot, and I wanted to have a Sebby somewhere in there too."

Sebastian's eyes watered. "That's perfect. Thank you, Fire. I'm honored."

Fire shrugged, ducking his head, suddenly feeling shy. "I love you."

Sebastian pulled him into a hug. "I love you too."

"We're going to enjoy her so much," Fire said, hugging Cyrus close. "Cy is gonna love her too."

Leti panted in the doorway. "Don't hold your breath. Rizzie and Sami fight all the time."

"They still love each other," Gram pointed out. "That's how Quigley and Sara were when they were younger. Love is a funny thing. By the time Sara was a teenager, they smoothed things out and were inseparable."

"Gods, I hope Rizzie and Sami will be like that. Pepper, Milo, and Elril love everyone, but those two know just how to annoy each other." Leti sniffed the air and went to get himself a cup of coffee. "I just told Shae the news. He's on his way."

Wolfe lounged in the doorway, eyes sparkling as he smirked.

"Hey, Wolfe." Fire waved Cyrus's little hand toward the former assassin. "You're back from where ever you went to spy on people."

"It's more interesting here," Wolfe signed, then moved silently through the kitchen to fetch his own cup of coffee.

The best word Fire could think of to describe Leti's friend was *quiet*, and not just because he couldn't speak. Wolfe reminded Fire a bit of Fluffle in how he moved silently through the neighborhood, keeping guard, always on the alert and ready to attack.

"You just like watching your friends do stupid things," Sebastian said, grinning. "Did you see Shae trip over Fluffle this morning and dump his coffee down Parker's back? That was fun."

"Friends are important," Fire said, biting his lip. He wanted all his babies to get along. Aster and David picked at one another, but they were friendly about it.

"That reminds me," Leti said, sitting next to Gram. "We're getting a new group of Burnished in about six months. They'll be training in engineering. Do you think Quig would mind spending some time with them once they get settled? I don't want them to feel out of place. They would probably like a friend from here."

"Living on a station is really different than living on Burnished Outpost," Fire said, tapping his chin. "Quigley and the kids get cold easily and had trouble adapting to longer lunar days."

"We can help them adjust," Leti said, sighing. "I'm always surprised so few of them want to stay here at the end of their training. I want them to have a positive experience of Charybdis Station."

"That's our Blue Angel talking," Sebastian said, smiling at Leti. "Always wanting to help."

Leti stuck his tongue out at Sebastian, making the rest of them laugh.

Fire grabbed a cup of tea, since he hated coffee, and sat beside Gram. His mornings had changed since getting a family, but they had changed for the better.

He handed Jellybean a plate with a sliced banana on it and watched his friend enjoy his snack. Fire wanted his mate to be as happy as he was. *I need to get Quig his desert sunrise.*

~

A COUPLE HOURS LATER, FIRE FINALLY MADE IT TO THE FULL Moon Sector of the station. His friend Beck lived with his mate, who happened to be the leader of the Full Moon assassins.

Fire stepped off the tram and bounced Cyrus in front of him, enjoying the baby's giggles. Beck and Beol lived at the center of the sector, so it wasn't hard to find their house.

Fire waved at the patrolling guards he saw. "We have more security now, Cy. Mean people keep getting on the station."

Beck was just leaving the house when Fire reached him.

The large green Grell smiled. "Hey, we have some tasty chicken in the fridge if you're hungry."

Dr. Bloop wore his going-out goggles perched between his ears. He sat beside his person and woofed softly. *Babies with little daddy*.

Fire giggled. He liked how Dr. Bloop called Beol *little daddy* and Beck *big daddy*. "I'm not here to play with the babies this time, Dr. Bloop. I need to ask Beck a favor."

Beck looked surprised. "What do you need?"

Fire swayed in place. "My mate is pregnant, and I want to get him a present."

CHAPTER 12

Quigley tugged the sleeve of his coat down a little farther. He had been extra cold today, though the temperature on Charybdis Station stayed the same, day or night. Quigley had been feeling *off* ever since Death had confirmed what he and Fire had suspected.

His bones weren't speaking to him either, but they had been quiet since he'd left Burnished Outpost. Gram told him he just needed to adjust to having a station under his feet instead of a planet.

"I'm pregnant." The words came out before he could stop them, and he quickly looked around, his bow slapping against his side at the movement.

Silas and he were patrolling a portion of the massive market area. Even early in the day, people crowded the area. Hack had explained that the station got many more tourists than it used to, so the market had grown over the past few years. There were also several guests visiting to tour the new university that weekend.

"There are so many people," he said, trying to keep the awe from his voice.

"You're pregnant?" Silas asked.

Quigley stopped walking and looked behind him. Silas stood frozen in place, staring at him.

"Is that a problem?" Quigley hadn't thought Silas would be the kind of person to care about it. "I'm still able to work."

Silas shook his head, finally unfreezing. "No, it's great news. I'm just surprised. You've only been mated a few months."

"It *was* a surprise," Quigley admitted, wincing. "I've known it was a possibility my whole life, but to actually have it happen is overwhelming."

Silas nudged him with his arm as they continued their patrol. "Especially with all the changes you've had the past few months. I'm still amazed you've adapted as quickly as you have."

"Some days I don't want to leave the house." Quigley flushed at the admission. Silas was too easy to talk with. "Surviving means adapting, so I've been pushing the kids and myself."

Their comms chimed with an incoming message. Quigley quickly read his. "Suspected theft."

"That booth is a few rows down," Silas said and led the way. "Tulah has several jewelry booths set up in the market, and there are a few nice pieces to tempt someone with sticky fingers."

A tall Siren with long white hair waited impatiently for them. She gripped the arm of a skinny young man that looked to be maybe sixteen. Quigley didn't recognize his species immediately.

"This ruffian stuffed several of my pieces in his pocket and tried to run." Tulah glared at the boy. He remained silent and stared at the ground.

Silas winced. "Why don't you run me through events,

Tulah. I'll go ahead and get the report going. My partner, Quigley, can handle the kid."

Tulah reluctantly let go of the boy, and Quigley led him away.

"What is your name?" Quigley asked, keeping his voice low. He had discovered during training that his size and deep voice could be intimidating to smaller species.

"Gavin Calla," the boy said, sniffling.

"Will you tell me what happened?" Quigley asked. He knew security would have footage of the events, but they needed to hear it from everyone.

The boy shrugged. "I grabbed some stuff and she caught me. Why is there a lizard on your head?"

"He's my friend," Quigley said. "Why did you try to take the jewelry?" Silas had explained that motive was always important to know even with the most obvious of crimes.

Gavin pressed his lips together and shook his head. "It doesn't matter."

"Yes, it does." Quigley sighed. "Okay, let's start from the beginning. What were you doing in the market?"

It took a full hour, but Quigley finally figured out Gavin had tried to steal the jewelry as gifts for his mother and sisters. They were among the many refuges that had recently moved to Charybdis Station.

"Tell Ms. Tulah what you told me," Quigley ordered. He braced his hands on the boy's slender shoulders. "The truth."

Gavin muttered under his breath. "Can't you just take me to a cell or something? I'd even take a shot from your bow. Why do you even have a bow?"

Tulah glared at them both.

"Gavin." Quigley used his Serious Dad voice. It always worked on David.

"Okay." Gavin groaned. "We don't have credits for

anything. Charybdis Station gives us the necessities, and Mom is *grateful*. I hate it. We had so much back on Rueal, and Dad had a good job, but he's dead and everything's gone. We lost everything, even Vetta's toys. I just wanted to get Mom and the girls something pretty."

Tulah's eyes narrowed. "You think that justifies stealing from me? I worked hard every day to build my business from *nothing*. My family went without so we could put every extra credit back into my creations. Just because you want something doesn't give you the right to take it."

Gavin gave her a sullen look. "I'm sorry."

"Don't you say that without meaning it." Tulah held up her arm and jingled the delicately made bangles that lined it. "You think pretty jewelry is what will make your family happy? Don't be stupid. They have you. They have each other. You aren't alone with no one to love you. That's what's important." She looked around. "Just don't tell my customers that."

Gavin ducked his head. "I'm really sorry, okay? I know I'm lucky to still have them. I used to complain about having three sisters, but now, I can't imagine not having them."

"Then don't risk a jail cell over something so stupid," Tulah said, looking like she wanted to smack Gavin atop the head. "Young ones these days have no sense."

Gavin groaned. "Mom's going to murder me."

Tulah huffed. "No, she won't because you're going to work my booth to *earn* some pretties for your mom and your sisters. When that's done, we'll see what you've learned. Maybe I'll keep you on or maybe I'll help you get work somewhere else. We'll see."

Gavin's mouth dropped open. "Seriously?"

Tulah gave him a hard look. "You do this, or I send you with enforcement."

"I'll work hard." Gavin stood up straight. "I swear."

"You'll probably wish I would have let them take you away." Tulah smirked. "There's a reason no one likes to work for me."

Silas sighed. "Did I write up this damn report for nothing?"

Tulah patted his cheek. "Work is good for you. It builds character."

Quigley hid his smile.

Tulah turned to him and eyed his ear cuffs. "Those are very nice. I like to see a warrior who appreciates the shiny things in life. I have some other designs that will suit you. They'll distract people from noticing the lizard on your head."

Quigley's eyes widened. "Uh, I'm actually working right now. I don't think I'm supposed to shop while—"

"I'll set them back and you can come by when your shift ends." Tulah waved them away. "Gavin will go to school now, since that's where he's supposed to be. He will report back here directly after."

"Yes, ma'am." Gavin nodded furiously. "I'll go right now."

"I'll find you if you don't come back." Tulah gave him a dark look. "You won't like what happens then."

Gavin squeaked. "I'll come back. I promise."

Quigley quickly followed Silas away from the booth. *Will she search for me if I don't come back?* He didn't really want to find out.

As soon as they were out of sight, Silas turned and grinned. "Good job, Quig."

"I think I'm expected to buy ear cuffs." He looked nervously over his shoulder, then patted Cinnamon's back.

Silas snorted. "Tulah can sniff out weakness from across

the station. She has good taste, though, and is a skillful artist. You'll like what she offers you."

Quigley sighed and stroked a finger down his ear. Fire wasn't one for jewelry since he was apt to shift into his elemental form at any time. He had taken great joy in buying things for Quigley, Gram, and the kids.

Quigley pushed the thought away and scanned the crowds around him. He thought about Gavin and his family. "Charybdis Station took in a lot of refuges."

"Yeah, and more are coming every day." Silas nodded to one of the venders. "The station is growing quickly, but the leadership can handle it."

"They take in the unloved and abandoned," Quigley said softly. "I think Fasi is Helara. Maybe Leti and Fire too. The whole station may really be Helara."

Silas gave him a puzzled look. "Huh?"

Quigley shrugged. "It's not important."

Silas shrugged. "So how do you feel about the baby?"

"Excited, worried, scared." Quigley smiled. "I felt the same when I first took in Aster. She was a tiny newborn, and I was just me. I thought it would be easier with David, but no. I still felt that surge of fear. The same happened with Cyrus. Now, with this one, at least I was expecting it."

Something flashed in Silas's eyes before he looked away. "I'm happy for you two."

Quigley frowned and pulled Silas to a stop. "What's wrong?"

Silas shook his head. "Nothing."

"Silas." Quigley used the Dad Voice again.

His friend winced. "That shouldn't work on me."

Quigley arched a brow.

"Okay, okay." Silas groaned and started walking again. "Rune and I want a baby. We've been trying for years, but it's just not going to happen. I'm shooting blanks, and all the treatments I've taken haven't done a bit of good."

Quigley started to speak, then stopped.

"I know there are a ton of kids we could adopt," Silas continued. "I know we could get a sperm donor. It's just… I wanted to be the one to give Rune a baby. I wanted to create something special together. I feel like I've failed him."

"Oryx shit," Quigley finally managed to say. "I know Rune, and he would never think that."

"Of course he doesn't," Silas said, rolling his eyes. "He's been completely understanding and supportive throughout everything. It's just what I feel, and I don't know how to fix it."

Quigley stayed quiet for a moment. "Maybe time's what you need. You had a dream that's not going to happen. Maybe you need time to adapt and change your dream. You have Rune. You and he *have* created something special. Start with that."

Silas gave him a half-smile. "Here we are talking about my woes when we should be celebrating your first day on enforcement and your pregnancy."

Quigley shrugged. "We're friends, Silas. Fire tells me that friends are always there for one another."

Silas gave him a look. "I'm glad you're Fire's lifemate. Not too many people would appreciate him for who he is."

Quigley ran a hand over his abdomen. "Death's worried that the station won't handle the news of my pregnancy well since Fire is a Crellic Element. I'm not worried though. Fire isn't like Death."

Silas snorted. "No, he isn't. The station knows it too. They see him as some friendly force of nature, not a threat."

"That's what he is," Quigley said, nodding.

Silas eyed him. "Some would complain because he has zero boundaries and a big mouth."

Quigley growled. "Some would get their ass kicked."

"True," Silas said with a grin. "Like I said, I'm glad you're the one his soul paired with."

Their comms chimed again, and Quigley smiled. *Time to work.*

CHAPTER 13

"I'm just saying, this group of Burnished was a lot smaller than I expected, and there's something different about them," Leti said, following along behind Fire. "They're not very friendly at all, and the pilot kept giving them strange looks. Plus, they got here a month early. I can't even get ahold of our contact on Burnished Outpost to ask about them because the stupid communications officer keeps transferring me to fudging Grellweir."

Fire ignored Leti and snapped the last latch into place. "How's it look, Shae?"

"Like a glass ball," Shae said dryly. He stood below them with Cyrus on his hip. "This is going to take a lot to maintain, Fire. Are you sure about this?"

"My love muffin deserves the best." Fire looked over the desert landscape they had created in the corner of their community park. It had been hard to hide it from Quigley, but they were finishing it today, so at least he wouldn't have to keep coming up with excuses to explain why it was walled off and covered up.

Cyrus held his arms out toward Fire. "Dada."

"Coming, baby boy." Fire paused beside Leti and hugged his friend. "Why don't you call Bowan? He said to call anytime."

"I know he *said* that but did he actually mean it?" Leti asked, huffing. "He has an advisor that handles the training trips, so I don't want to go over his head by going to Bowan."

"Little trouble," Shae said, nodding to the side.

They all turned to watch Milo crawl onto Princess Buttercup's back. Leti's youngest was getting adventurous a little too quickly for everyone's peace of mind.

Several of the other pets watched from where they lay in the desert sand. *Little dragon wants to ride*, Chutney explained to Fire, his meows deep and quiet.

"Milo, no rides without an adult present." Leti groaned and ran to them. "I'll be back later."

Fire snickered when Princess grew a bit larger to accommodate them for a ride. Princess loved flying with Leti and Milo.

Wanna fly. Jellybean rolled past him in his ball. *I need wings.*

"Sorry, Jellybean. I don't think guinea pigs can grow wings." Fire gave Shae a questioning look, and his friend shook his head. "Nope. Shae says they don't."

Stupid. Jellybean squeaked loudly and rolled away.

Wobble and Cactus stopped beside him to say hello. The Oryx nosed Fire's pocket until he pulled out a treat. "Here you go." Wobble gave him a look, and he sighed before giving him one too. "Leti said I'll make you both fat."

Mother is wrong, Wobble said before nudging Cactus. *To flowers, brother.*

The two wandered back to the open gate leading into their pasture.

"Okay, that should do it." Beck moved to stand beside

him. He stared at his tablet for a moment. "The metal divider cuts this little patch off from the rest of the park. Pops and I gave your desert hideaway its own shields and temperature control. We've triple checked the connections, and the artificial sun is ready to go. It'll brighten and dim with the rest of the station's schedule. If we were a little closer to the system's sun, we wouldn't have to even worry about it, but that's what we get for parking the station at the edge of the system."

"Why'd we have to be way out here anyway?" Fire asked, huffing as he tromped through the sand.

"Because it's not in any other planet's space." Shae sighed. "Sand is ridiculous."

"When is Quig getting home?" Beck asked, rubbing his stomach. "I'm hungry."

"In an hour," Fire said, checking the time on his comm. "Thanks, Beckie-Boo."

Beck groaned. "Don't call me that."

"Are we too late?" Sebastian asked, running through the green portion of the community park, Kelly on his heels. "Kelly had the best idea."

Fire scowled. "No, it's stupid."

"You don't even know what it is." Kelly smirked. "That's why I'm not going to ask. I'm just going to do it."

"Is it hooked up?" Sebastian asked, face excited.

"Yep," Beck said, grinning proudly. "Pops is bringing the stands now. We'll put it up right here."

"We have a better idea," Sebastian said, smiling at Kelly. He plucked a seed from his pocket and buried it in the sand next to the large contraption before dumping some water on it. "Show them what all that practice taught you."

Kelly held out her hand and focused. A moment later, she glowed with a soft green and gold light.

"What are you doing?" Fire asked, looking at the buried seed.

A small sprout popped from the ground. Slowly, it grew larger and larger until a small tree with rough bark stood in its place. Gradually, the tree expanded, growing taller as the trunk grew thicker.

Branches started to form, and two of them smoothly reached around Beck's contraption and slowly lifted it by its base as the tree continued to grow. The branches twisted and adjusted to settle the large, circular device at the center of the tree.

Then it grew and grew and grew.

After about ten minutes, the tree was over thirty feet high and had beautiful purple and green foliage. Six bare branches extended high above the leaves like a hand. A hand that held the base of Beck's artificial sun.

Kelly groaned as she lowered her hand. "Why is it so hared to control one tree's growth?"

Sebastian wrapped an arm around Fire's shoulder. "What do you think?"

Fire's lip trembled. "It's perfect."

Beck whistled, eyes wide in shock. "I'll never get used to what you shamans can do. That looks a sight prettier than the metal frame we planned."

Fire sniffed and wiped his eyes. "I still hate you, Kelly."

She grinned and leaned over to kiss his cheek. "I hate you too."

"Hello, hello," Ma called out across the park. "Juniper and I have the food."

Fire's stomach grumbled, telling him that food would be really good.

"Dada," Cyrus said, voice small. He held his arms out to Fire.

"Oh, baby boy, I'm sorry I forgot you wanted me." Fire took him from Shae. "Mean Aunt Kelly distracted me."

"Aww, I'm *Aunt* Kelly now," Kelly said, smiling.

"My goodness," Ma said walking closer. She stared at the large tree. "I've never seen a tree like that before."

"It's a common tree from Burnished Outpost," Kelly said, plopping down in one of the lounge chairs nearby. "Special ordered the seed."

Ma shook her head, a look of wonder on her face. "The things I see at this place."

Shae's comm chimed, and he frowned at it before pushing a button. "Leti?"

"I think there might be a problem." Leti's voice was small and echoey through the communicator. "Milo and I are up high, and I was looking down and saw the new group of Burnished entering the neighborhood. They're going straight for Fire and Quig's house."

"They want to visit?" Fire looked at Ma. "Do we have enough food?"

"I don't think they want to visit," Leti said. "They're armed, and some are already glowing like Hack does before he draws on his fire."

Fire narrowed his eyes, all Leti's worries suddenly making perfect sense. "I gotta see them."

"Huh?" Shae asked, staring at him as he walked away. "Where are you going?"

Fire paused as he passed Juniper and took one of the little sandwiches on the tray his friend carried. "I love chicken salad."

"Fire." Sebastian sounded frustrated. "What's going on?"

Fire ate the sandwich in a few bites, then handed Cyrus to Shae. "Guard my son. I think I'm gonna have to go Fluffle on some people."

Shae sighed. "I'll keep Cyrus safe. Let me know if you need help. I wish Wolfe were here, but no, he had to go spy for the station."

Fire pushed out his chest. "I have to protect my family myself."

Gram looked up from her cup of coffee. She sat at one of the picnic tables on the green side of the park. "What's this about protecting the family?"

Fire ignored her and went to the edge of the park, peeking around a large oak. "It *is* him."

A group of six Burnished walked toward his house. They were strapped down with weapons, and two of them already had balls of fire in their hands.

Leading them was the horrible, mean little man from the desert. The one that wanted to kill Quigley and Cyrus.

"What is Dustin doing here?" Gram said, voice panicked. "How did he even get off of Burnished Outpost?"

"Enemies?" Beck asked, moving to stand next to him. The others gathered around and stared at the group. So far, they hadn't been spotted, but the park was right across from their house, so it wouldn't be long.

"Bad guys." Fire took a breath. "I'll take care of it. I should have… I should have killed them from the beginning."

"They killed my Sara." Gram's voice was thick with tears. "She just wanted to protect Cyrus, and they killed her."

"I'll take care of it." Fire blinked away his tears. He hated the smell of burnt flesh and the screams people made. He hated knowing his flames caused the permanent ending of another being. The queen had made him kill so many.

"Not this time," Kelly said, voice hard. She held her hand out and began to glow green and gold again.

"Agreed." Sebastian extended his own hand, the aura around him flickering from red and gold to green and brown. "You take the back three. Just like we trained last month."

"On it." Kelly squinted, and Fire felt a push of energy leave her.

The three men at the back of the group yelped when vines grew from the ground around them and twisted around their legs. In seconds, they were completely covered, and Fire heard a sickening crunch as their bones cracked when the vines constricted.

Dustin and the remaining two spun around to stare at their dead friends.

Dustin raised his hands, and his inner flames grew brighter in the palm of his hands.

"You said the others lied," one man accused. "You said the gods didn't chase you through the desert. Now, they use the earth to kill us."

"You won't harm my family," Sebastian said, snarling.

He held out his hand, and the dirt beneath the remaining men whirled up from beneath the grass. It spun around the three men for a moment, then separated and shot to their faces. Dustin's flames surged and grew larger as dirt poured into his mouth and nostrils.

His flames faded as he lost consciousness and fell to the ground. The two others quickly followed suit, and seconds later, their bodies stilled.

Fire looked away from the dead. *At least wasn't my fire,* he thought, sniffling.

"It's over," Gram said quietly a moment later.

"I've called enforcement," Ma said, voice grim.

"Leti said that he sent Hack a message too." Shae bounced Cyrus in his arms. He kept the baby turned away so he wouldn't see the grisly sight across the street.

Jellybean rolled between Shae's legs and went straight to

Fire. He picked up his ball and hugged it to his chest. "I'm sorry, Gram. I'm sorry I didn't protect us."

Kelly spun around, glaring at him. "This isn't about protecting your family, Fire. If you had to, of course you could have taken care of those men."

Sebastian rubbed his back. "You *would* have too, sweetheart. We all know that."

Gram took a deep breath and let it out. "Kelly and Sebastian are right. This wasn't about you protecting your family. This was about ending a threat. It's done, and that's all that matters."

Fire squeezed his eyes shut. "I should have—"

"No," Gram said, moving close to hug him. "You're the *heart* of our family, Fire. You protect us all in a very different way. Today, Kelly and Sebastian protected you from having to do something that pains you."

"You have your own purpose, Fire. You make us happy." Kelly smacked his arm. "You make us smile."

"You give us love," Shae said, sighing. "You're a good friend, Fire. If we need you, you're always there."

"I love that you live life to the fullest," Juniper said, arms crossed. "You love food, pets, and babies, and see no shame in doing exactly what you want."

"You have no malice in you," Ma said, giving him a soft look. "How you've lived through what you have and carry no hatred in ya, I'll never understand. I'll just be happy for it."

"You give love easily," Beck said with a grin. "I've never made friends as easy as you, but I swear anyone that meets you loves you."

Sebastian hugged him. "You are a beautiful soul that offers us all so much joy. You're not a weapon, Fire, and we will *never* let you become one."

"Never." Gram joined the hug. "You're our beautiful Helara, and we'll always cherish you."

Fire let his tears fall and enjoyed his friends' hugs. *Even Kelly's.* "I don't want Quig to see them there."

Beck let him go and grabbed his comm. "Okay. I'll call maintenance to get rid of them."

"I'm telling Silas to keep Quigley late," Shae said and passed Cyrus to Fire. "The kids won't be back for another few hours, so we should have everything ready by then."

"Juniper and I will set things up and take care of the food so it doesn't spoil," Ma said, kissing the top of Fire's head. "You have a man to impress tonight."

"Not like you have to do much," Gram said, rolling her eyes. "You smile and he comes running."

Fire hugged Cyrus. "Are you hungry, baby boy? Grandpa Sebby will help us make a bottle."

Sebastian shuddered. "Please don't call me Grandpa Sebby."

CHAPTER 14

Quigley frowned at the Burnished pilot. "Charles, you weren't scheduled to be here for another month, and Chieftain Bowan said the trainee group hasn't even left Burnished Outpost. You're supposed to be patrolling in the southern hemisphere."

The man in front of them glared at Quigley's obviously pregnant abdomen. He had started showing about two months ago and now had a nice-sized baby bump.

"I brought some trainees early. That's all." Charles crossed his arms and looked away.

Renee snorted. "I went to your *trainees'* quarters, and they weren't there. In fact, they haven't checked in with their instructors at all in the two days they've been here. Something's going on, and you're going to tell us what it is."

"I don't have to entertain your paranoia." The man gave Quigley a disgusted look. "I shouldn't even have to be in the same room as this disgrace."

Quigley sighed and exchanged a look with Silas. They both moved to grab one of Renee's arms when she rushed forward.

"Listen here, asshole," Renee said, vibrating with anger. "That's my grandbaby growing in there. I will cut your fucking tongue out and shove it up your—"

"You might consider answering our questions before we let her go," Silas interrupted with a grin. His fangs flashed in the overhead light.

Cinnamon chose that moment to peek out of Quigley's unruly curls and hiss at Charles.

Charles's face drained of color. "That's a black stinger. Keep it away."

"Don't worry about the damn lizard," Renee said, growling. "Worry about me."

Charles shook. "No one said Quigley was related to the Chief of Enforcement and the Lord Admiral."

"Why was anyone discussing me?" Quigley asked, suddenly having the urge for some jerky. Gram made the best rabbit jerky, but the only rabbit close to them was Mo's pet, Abbot, and there was no way Quigley was catching and eating a pet, especially not one that visited Fire every morning for a lettuce nibble break.

Renee's comm chimed, and they reluctantly let her go. She pulled it from her pocket and read whatever message was urgent enough for communications to interrupt their interview.

"Charles," Silas said. "Continue."

Charles looked conflicted for a moment, then seemed to make up his mind. "My cousin married into your old clan. Dustin is the new clan elder since your sister murdered his father."

Thoughts of jerky disappeared, and Quigley leaned forward. "Go on."

"Dustin can't let his wife's betrayal go," Charles said, swallowing hard. "It's a dishonor."

"There is no way anyone of my previous clan would get on a ship," Quigley said, shaking his head. "What do they have to do with the trainees that aren't trainees?"

"Dustin *did* get on a ship," Charles said, biting his lip. "He brought five of his best warriors with him. They know where you live, everyone does. They're going to kill his welp. It's *his* right, and you took that away from him. He wants to kill you too, but we weren't sure if he could manage both."

Cyrus. Quigley turned for the door. He felt Cinnamon scrambling to keep his balance.

Renee grabbed his arm. "Wait. That message was from Leti. The threat is over. This Dustin asshole and his warriors are dead. Cy and Fire are okay."

"They're dead?" Charles looked horrified.

"You shouldn't worry about them," Renee said, smiling sweetly. "You're mine now, asshole. You commit a crime on Charybdis Station and you lose any diplomatic rights. Bowan will understand."

Quigley didn't stay to hear the man's pleas. He hurried from the room and through the halls of the Enforcement Headquarters.

Silas followed behind him, looking at his own comm. "Oh shit. Uh, Quigley, I'm supposed to distract you for another hour."

Quigley stopped and turned. He stared at Silas, brow arched.

Silas shrugged. "It's what Fire wants. He doesn't want you to see the bodies, so they're cleaning them up."

"I'm not sitting on my ass while my mate suffers."

"He's fine," Silas said, shrugging.

"He never wanted to kill anyone ever again." Quigley shook his head, anger bubbling up. "I brought trouble to his door and ruined it."

Silas blinked. "He, uh, didn't kill them. From what Shae said in his message, Sebastian and Kelly kicked ass. They didn't give Fire the chance to do anything."

Quigley felt a smile slowly crawl across his face. "They did?"

Silas nodded. "Now, why don't we go pick up the kids? You know Fire likes cuddles, and they'll make him happy."

Quigley sighed. "Okay, but I want some jerky too, and maybe some goat milk."

Silas wrinkled his nose. "Yeah, sure. Jerky and goat milk."

❧

"SO DUSTIN IS DEAD?" DAVID ASKED, LEANING INTO Quigley's side. His son liked whispering to Quigley's baby bump often, so he could usually be found near Quigley's stomach when they were together.

"He is," Quigley answered, walking slowly to the house. His mate wanted time, so Quigley was doing his best. The stop for food and to pick up the kids hadn't taken as long as Silas would have liked.

Aster walked on his other side, her hand in his. "Good. He deserved it for killing Aunt Sara."

"Oh, thank the stars," Silas muttered when they drew close to home. There were no bodies or anything really to suggest a struggle had taken place in front of their house.

Fire and Cyrus were watching them through the front window. Something eased in Quigley when he saw his mate's smile. *He can't be too upset if he's smiling like that.* Fire wasn't exactly adept at hiding his emotions.

Fire opened the front door and handed him Cyrus. "Our baby is okay."

"I never thought he wouldn't be." Quigley leaned down and kissed Fire, taking the time to run his tongue between Fire's lips and taste him.

"Ugh," David said. "Aster, they're kissing."

"You didn't *have* to tell me," she said, pushing David's shoulder.

"If I have to know, you have to know." David ran for the kitchen. "Where's Gracie? I need to tell her about school."

Aster sighed and moved deeper into the house. "The goat better not be in the house again."

Quigley leaned back, breaking their kiss. "I missed you."

"I always miss you," Fire said, pouting. "Cy and I should be able to go to work with you."

Cy leaned up and gave Quigley a slobbery baby kiss on his chin. "Dada."

"I'm glad you two are alright." Quigley let the guilt fill him. He preferred to face his feelings head-on instead of ignoring them. "I'm sorry I brought all of this to you."

Fire snorted. "Silly mate. You've only ever brought me happy times, even though you stole Cinnamon and break my pretty underwear all the time."

"They like it when I do that," Quigley said, smiling against Fire's neck.

"That's what you say, but Death says he never knew anyone who can talk to underwear." Fire patted Quigley's baby bump. "Are you hungry?"

"Do we have any jerky?" Quigley tried for a pitiful look. "Maybe some potatoes?"

Fire gave him a suspicious look. "Mo said you were looking funny at Abbot yesterday. Plus, Abbot told me that you commented on the size of his haunches."

Quigley smiled, going for innocent this time. "I have no idea what they're talking about."

"You're lucky we got Ma and Juniper," Fire said, pulling him toward the door. "They made all kinds of yummy stuff. I'll get you a plate after you see your surprise."

"What surprise?" Quigley's mouth watered as he thought of platters of delicious food.

"Dad, Gracie and all the food is at the park," David yelled, running in from the backyard. "I'm gonna go get Aster."

Quigley watched Fire. "Hmm, now I really need to know what the surprise is. It can't be the food because they feed us all the time."

Fire gave him a shy smile and pulled him out the front door. "I wanted you to have desert sunrises and sunsets, so your bones will talk to you again and you'll be happy."

Quigley shook his head. "All I need to be happy is you, little flame. You're more beautiful and special to me than all the sunrises and sunsets in existence."

"Don't talk so pretty," Fire said, giving him a heated look. "We can't be naughty right now."

Quigley started to say something but forgot everything when he saw the mini desert at the opposite edge of the park. It was about an acre and looked like it was plucked from Burnished Outpost. At the center of the desert was a large spiny snake tree. Its thin, center branches held a brightly shining circular orb.

As soon as sand was under his feet, his bones seems to sigh in relief. He had known he missed Burnished Outpost, but he hadn't realized how much.

"What's going on?" he asked, looking around at the people gathered around them. The kids were back from school, and most of their neighbors and friends were there.

Silas patted his shoulder. "Fire wanted something special for you."

"We built you a sun," Beck said, grinning proudly. "It'll rise and set with the station's public lighting settings."

Kelly waved her hands across the sand. "Over this lovely little dessert that we've named the Kelly Desert."

"We didn't name it that," Fire said, sticking his tongue out at his arch-nemesis.

Sebastian rolled his eyes. "What they're saying is that every morning and evening, you can come here to get your fill of desert sunrises and sunsets. Sheesh, these two are worse than Rizzie and Sami."

Quigley blinked back his tears. "Fire, you did all this for me?"

Fire gave him a nervous look. "Do you like it?"

Quigley pulled him into his arms. "I love it, Fire. I love you for thinking of this. The sand under my feet is exactly what I needed."

David and Aster sat in the sand, twin looks of wonder on their faces. Jellybean rolled down a hill, building up speed before crashing into Shae.

Fire held Cyrus close and watched Quigley, love in his eyes.

This is Helara. It has to be, Quigley thought.

Gram huffed and gave Quigley a knowing look. "He's our heart, isn't he?"

Quigley nodded, unable to find the right words. He stared into Fire's swirling eyes. "You're my Helara. The heart of my clan. My little flame."

EPILOGUE

FIVE YEARS LATER

Sara dragged Cyrus behind her as she ran down the street. "Seshi! We need you," she yelled at the top of her lungs.

Gretty and her best friend Hazel paused in their game of chase to stare at them, but Sara didn't stop to say hi like she normally would. "It's an urgency, Seshi!"

Cyrus laughed and flipped one of her curls in her face. "He can't hear ya. He's like a thousand steps away."

Sara blew hard and the curl bounced back, covering Cinnamon again. Daddy said she had her papa's hair, and she was starting to understand why he kept it short. Cinnamon liked living on her head though. Papa said it was because her hair looked like a black stinger nest.

She skidded to a stop, her clomping boots keeping her upright. *Doin' their job*, she thought with a grin.

Cyrus was a lot more graceful with his own stop. "Why we got to run all the time? David says you wouldn't need the ugly boots if you didn't run all the time."

"Shut it. I love my clomping boots," Sara said, running

into Seshi's backyard. That was where she could usually find their best friend. "Seshi, we need you."

Seshi looked up, his eerie black eyes dancing with amusement. "What did you break this time?"

Sara fell into a sprawl next to him, pulling Cyrus down with her. She handed the box to Seshi. "Aster's music box fell off the dresser when Cy ran into it."

"I ran into it 'cause you was pulling me around," Cyrus said, rolling his eyes. "Can you fix it, Seshi? This is the one Xu gave Aster on their first date. She listens to it all the time."

Seshi looked it over, poking and prodding it with his driver. "I can fix it. Give me a little time."

Sara groaned and flopped back in the grass, barely missing Seshi's dog, Midge. "My life's over. Aster's gonna kill me if you don't hurry, and she'll let Wooley eat me."

"Daddy and Papa won't let her kill you," Cyrus said, voice worried. "David says they like you a little."

"They have another baby," Sara said, working up to a wail. "Petey is nicer than me."

Seshi chuckled. "Jellybean says they won't let Aster get rid of you. He remembers when you were born and says your daddies were really happy."

"Thanks, Jellybean," she said, sighing heavily. A familiar weight pressed into her side, and she patted at the guinea pig spirit.

A shadow passed overhead, and she sat up quickly, picking up Jellybean and holding him against her chest. "I got to go, guys. Princess is calling."

Cyrus laughed and felt around until he could grab Jellybean. "Remember to take off the boots. You cried last time you burnt them."

Sara vibrated in place as she pulled off her boots and

dress. Her friends were used to her undressing and didn't pay her any mind as she shifted into her elemental form.

Her body melted away and all she was became a small ribbon of flames. She shot through the air and caught up with Princess Buttercup. She flew beside him as they headed around the neighborhood.

"Hey, Sara," Milo said, waving from the back of the Fire Veil dragon. It was just him, so he'd get in trouble with his daddies. He wasn't supposed to ride without an adult.

Sara pushed the worry away. Flying was for fun, not worries.

BOOKS BY C. W. GRAY

Writing as C.W. Gray

- **Charybdis Station Chronicles** – *science fiction/fantasy, mpreg*

The Blue Solace Series – Books One - Seven
Charybdis Station

- **The Hobson Hills Omegas** – non-shifter, mpreg, omegaverse
- Additional Books:
- "The Beta's Love Song"
- "Bennett's Dream"
- "Justin's Journey"
- "Grey's Gift"
- *Hobson Hills Shorts: Volume One*
- "Zoe's Happily Ever After"
- **Holiday Omegas Shorts** – holiday short stories from the world of The Silver Isles – paranormal, mpreg, omegaverse

Sonny and Leo (Anthology with books 1-4)

- **The Silver Isles** – paranormal, mermen, mpreg, omegaverse
- Additional Book
- "A Mate from the Deep"

Writing as Chloe Gray

- **A Little Bit of Perfect** – contemporary, non-mpreg, Daddy/Little age play

If you would like to keep up with releases, please like and follow me on my Facebook author page, join C.W. Gray's Reading Nook on Facebook, or visit my website at (https://www.cwgray-author.com).

www.ingramcontent.com/pod-product-compliance
Lightning Source LLC
Chambersburg PA
CBHW050003040726
47599CB00014B/1191